The Christmas Diary

A Novella by
Rebecca Buckley

First Printing November 2013

For information about special discounts for bulk purchases, please contact the publisher at: rjbpublishing@aol.com.

ISBN: 978-0-9891200-8-1

R. J. Buckley Publishing
San Tan Valley, AZ
rjbuckleypublishing.com
rjbpublishing@aol.com

Also by Rebecca Buckley

NOVELS - Rachel O'Neill Series

Midnight at Trafalgar
Midnight at the Eiffel
Midnight in Brussels
Midnight in Moscow
Midnight in Malibu

COLLECTIONS - Stories and Plays

Love Has a Price Tag
Bits & Pieces of Me
My Dramedy
Shoe's on the Other Foot

"In the United States today, there are nearly 13.6 million single parents raising over 21 million children."

To My Daughter Tami Jo

PART ONE

Mama's Diary

1

Christmas Eve in intensive care is never the choice for anybody. It should be a joyous, glorious occasion. But this one was not.

Lydia Howard opened her eyes and looked up as the nurse handed the pink fabric-covered book to her daughter.

Lydia's voice was weak, almost inaudible, just above a whisper, "I couldn't wrap it for you ... Honey ... nurse put ribbon ... and ornament on it ... did it up real pretty ... didn't she?" Lydia's eyelids closed slightly, hanging there as if they were tired and couldn't stay open.

"Oh, Mama, I didn't expect a present from you, but it's so beautiful! The pink flowers, the ribbon, the bell. So pretty. Thank you so much." Honey nodded her thanks to the nurse before she turned to leave the room to attend to her other patients. Then she kissed her mother on the forehead. "I love you, Mama."

"It's special, Honey ... one of my diaries ... my very special Christmas diary ... things I couldn't say to you. Read last page aloud." She spoke to her daughter in a raspy voice, her eyes glistening through her eyelashes. "Go ahead, Honey ... I'm listening."

Not a nickname, Honey was her real name. Honey Ray Howard, initials H.R.H. Ever since Honey was a child she had been teased and called H.R.H. - *Her Royal Highness* - her Mama always called her Honey, the name she gave her at birth, her only child.

It not only was Christmas Eve, you see, it was Honey's birthday too, she was born on Christmas Eve thirty-two years ago - a Christmas baby.

"Go on now ... read ... my last present to you."

"Don't say that, Mama." Honey's emotions were scrambling at the surface trying to burst through. She kept the tears from running down her cheeks with her sweater sleeve. "Why the last page, Mama?" she asked, her wavering voice giving away her feelings.

"You'll see. Start from where ... where I drew the star." She began coughing, not able to catch her breath.

Honey panicked. "Should I get the nurse?"

"No, no. I'm alright. Go on, read it, please."

Honey began reading out loud, *"Today, my dearest, darling child was born. It is Christmas Eve, December 24, 1979. They just came back in and took her away to give me a rest. I have all I ever wanted."*

Honey stopped reading. More tears filled her eyes as she looked at her mama lying in the hospital bed. Lydia Howard was a fragile shell of the person she had always

2

been. Always a strong woman, small in stature, but a force to contend with - her peers could attest to that. She started coughing again.

"Can I get you something, Mama? What should I do?"

Lydia shook her head as the coughing became harder and coarser. She was suffering from inoperable lung cancer and drowning in her own fluid.

The nurse hurried in and reached for the suction device.

"Is she all right?" Honey asked, frowning and frantic.

"Just need to fix her up, she'll be good as new."

"Should I leave?"

"No, you're just fine."

Christmases were always the hardest for Honey when she was growing up. All her friends had both parents with brothers and sisters to celebrate the family holidays. It was a double whammy because Christmas was her birthday too. She envied her friends' family parties and the tons of presents they opened together on birthdays and at Christmas. For her, it was always just she and her mother during the holidays, no other family. Even as an adult she felt like something was missing during the holiday season, but she would tell herself: *Christmases are for children. Get over it.* She also told herself if she ever had a child there would be a father and an extended family; it would make up for all the Christmases her mama and she spent alone.

She supposed that was the reason she loved doing things for less fortunate children as often as she could, especially during the holidays. It gave her some semblance of family togetherness she missed so much. Single-parent organizations were her focus, and for years she helped local groups give poverty-stricken families Thanksgiving and Christmas dinners and gifts of toys and clothing. Many times she was there in person to see the brightened faces of the little ones as they opened their presents, and the grateful faces of the parents accepting the dinners. It took so little of her time and money to help make that happen.

And here it was, Christmas again, the odds were that it was the last one she would spend with her mother. This time it was the unhappiest one of all. She had been in the hospital by her mama's side for nearly two weeks.

"Honey, are you there?" Lydia asked, exhausted after her bout of coughing.

The nurse was rinsing out equipment in the bathroom.

"I'm here, Mama. Right here beside you."

"Just going to take a little nap ... don't go away."

"I won't. I'll stay right here," Honey said choking back the sob that was trying to escape. When her mama was gone, she had nobody. No family at all.

Oh yes, she questioned her mama plenty of times about her father over the years, but there weren't any answers. A shrug of the shoulders was the most she ever got and no one else seemed to know anything either.

Honey didn't look like her mother. Honey had dark hair and green eyes, Lydia was blonde with blue eyes.

Lydia was small; Honey was tall. By the time Honey was thirteen years old, she was 5'9". She grew to 5'11" by the time she was eighteen. Not the most sought after girl in school at that height.

When she was a teenager and learned more about how women got pregnant, she came to the conclusion that maybe her mama didn't know who the father was. So she quit asking, not wanting to embarrass her. Something inside of her said '*don't put pressure on your mama.*' Besides she figured surely her mother would tell her if she knew, and then again, maybe Honey didn't need to know. She had her mama and that was all she needed. But her mama didn't know about the nights Honey cried herself to sleep because the kids at school had taunted her about not having a father.

Now Mama was dying. Now she wouldn't have a mama either.

As she watched her mama sleep, Honey thought back … *she was there for me on my first day of school right on up through high school. She was there for me when I graduated from Harvard. She was there for me through a relationship that went south, deep south. And she was there when my first novel became a best-seller, the novel that changed our lives and made it much easier for us.*

Mama's voice interrupted her reverie, "Go back to the beginning … and read a little bit."

"Okay, Mama." Honey picked up the diary and began reading again.

"*I have wanted a child of my own for as long as I can remember. I've wanted to know how it would feel to give birth to a baby.*"

Honey smiled and reached over and stroked her mama's arm, she looked like she'd fallen asleep again.

Lydia had worked her way up in the school system from teaching at high school level to becoming a principal of a middle school. The middle school served the small communities on the Central Coast of California - towns snuggling the coastline halfway between Los Angeles and San Francisco.

Honey's memories went back to growing up in Morro Bay as she watched her mama sleep.

The only time Honey lived away from California was while she was at Harvard. Her mama wanted her to become an attorney. She guessed that was because her mama always wanted to be one. So, she got the degree from Harvard for Mama, but she had no intention of becoming a lawyer, not in the least. She couldn't fathom having to speak and perform in front of a courtroom full of spectators, much less in front of a judge and other lawyers. It just wasn't in her. She was so glad to be out of school when she graduated with honors. It was all for her mother. Honey wanted to be a writer. She had wanted to write since she was a little girl reading her mama's books in her mama's worn, overstuffed chair. Luckily the local newspaper hired Honey after college, and she continued working there while freelancing – writing articles for every magazine that would publish her – while writing her first novel. Now her tenth novel had just been published and six of them had been on the N. Y. Times Bestseller List.

She continued to watch her mama lying in the hospital bed with her eyes closed, *she looks peaceful.*

"Go on, read some more, Honey. I'm not asleep."

"You could've fooled me," she laughed, knowing her mama had been asleep. She shifted in the chair and began reading the handwritten pages again.

"*Yes, I want my own little baby girl. I want to feel her tiny fingers gripping mine and want to rock her in a rocking chair and sing to her like mothers do in the movies. I have always wanted a little girl to dress up in frilly, lacy dresses that I never wore as a child. My childhood was drab and sad. So I have always wanted my own dear, dear daughter in the worst way to give her a life I didn't have.*"

Honey wiped her eyes with a tissue and covered her mouth and chin that were trembling uncontrollably. She didn't know much about her mother's upbringing, but she knew it had to have been unhappy by the mentions she would drop from time to time.

She did know her mama was named Lydia Jane by her father because her mother had died in childbirth. Lydia was raised by a strict father and stepmother, but at age nine she was sent to live with a distant cousin. Honey had always wondered why he sent Lydia away, and one day she asked her mama. She said she didn't know. Honey could see at the time how it had pained her mama to even talk about it, so she never brought it up again.

It was so difficult for Honey to read about the love her own mama felt for her even before she was born, and how much her mama had wanted her. What a contrast to the way Lydia must have felt growing up! How many children have that kind of mother's love? Honey had always felt it, had never doubted it, she had been her mama's whole world.

Looking closely at her mama while caressing her hair, Honey couldn't bear the thought of being without her. *I'm not ready, I need more time. We've always been together. What will I do?* The dread was starting. The pain was already stabbing at Honey's heart. *How can I live without this loving creature who has been my entire life? She is who I am, without her I am not. Who will I turn to when I need my mama? Who can I talk to about the craziness in my life, the decisions I need to make? Who? I have nobody.*

"Keep reading, Honey." Lydia turned over on her side, her eyes still closed as she broke into her daughter's deep thoughts.

"You want me to fix your pillow, Mama?"

"No, just keep reading to me, dear. I'm listening."

Honey gently held her mama's hand, feeling her frailness as she remembered when her first novel made the New York Times list. She built mama's dream house on the side of a hill overlooking the sea. They took summer vacations together, to Canada like mama always wanted, a cruise to Alaska included. Honey wanted her to have all she'd ever dreamed of having.

"Please ... I want to hear ... to re-live." Lydia's voice seemed weaker.

Honey took a deep breath and continued: "*I have prayed long and hard to have a baby. I believe in the Mary and Joseph story about Jesus, even though there are those who say it isn't true, that the story was concocted by religion, that there was no immaculate conception. It was all a fabrication by the church. Well, the birth of Baby Jesus is a beautiful story regardless. But no matter how hard I pray for it to happen to me, nothing happens – no repeat immaculate conception."*

Honey chuckled at her mama's humor.

"So I think I should take the matter into my own hands if I am to ever have a precious wee one to cuddle and raise as my own. Adoption agencies don't accept a single mother's application, so that leaves me with only one choice. Besides I want my own flesh and blood child."

Honey hesitated and darted a look at her mama.

"I'm listening," Lydia said, and coughed without opening her eyes.

"Is this going to tell me who my father is, Mama?" Honey's heart was pounding, she could feel her blood pressure rising. Her face was hot. "Is it?" Her voice was nearly a shriek.

"Read on and see." Lydia looked up at her, sort of mischievous-like.

"I'm not sure I want it to happen like this, after all these years," Honey said, especially with her mama on her deathbed, which she didn't say. It frightened her.

"Go on."

Suddenly Honey felt anxiety of another nature.

"The best candidate to make a baby is probably one of the teachers I work with who has been after me. But I think that's too close to home and I don't necessarily want to be married to him. I was married once and it was the most miserable time I ever had. So no, no more marriage.

9

Besides, I want a handsome man as well as an intellectual, so that eliminates the school teacher. He may be intellectual, but he's a little twerp, always blowing his nose and looking at the snotty handkerchief afterwards, and he scratches his crotch a lot, in public."

Honey laughed out loud. Lydia could be funny; her daughter loved that about her.

"The really good looking men I know are either married or queer, so I'm thinking about going on holiday to another country and having a fling. An out and out fling! I've seen romantic movies about that. No ties and far from home. Yes, that will work."

"Mama! You didn't?" Honey was laughing.

Lydia smiled innocently; her graying blond curls spread on the pillow, her eyes still closed. She looked like an angel lying there. She giggled. "Yes, I did ... your father ... most fabulous man ... I ever knew. Go on."

Honey was feeling excitement now. The fear was dissipating. Now she was eager to know. She read the opposite page.

"It's January of my sabbatical year and after wasting four months trying to get up the nerve to go to England by myself, I'm there. I met Gregory in a little fishing village in Cornwall called Weymouth.

"Weymouth is more of a working man's village, or town, actually. Not as upscale and touristy as Bournemouth and Southampton. As a matter of fact, Weymouth is larger than a village, has a shopping mall and all that - not like our shopping malls, but called that all the same. It's a town, actually; villages only have a few shops and a

grocer, a pub and a post office.

"So, Weymouth is a fishing town, and Gregory is a fisherman. The first days I was here I walked along the quay to breathe in the marvelous sea air and watch the fishing boats unload their daily catches. Most times I sit on the harbor wall and have a crab sandwich from the George Inn.

"One day Gregory came out of the George Inn across from where I was sitting, I didn't know him then. He was carrying two beer steins filled to the brim, and he asked me if he could join me. Said he'd be honored if I would relieve him of one of the drinks he was carrying. Of course, he wasn't really a two-fisted drinker; he had brought the drink to me purposefully. As it turns out, he'd been watching me every day that first week. Going to the George at lunch for a sandwich and sitting outside watching the gulls and the fishermen had become a habit for me."

Honey looked up from the diary, eyes wide.

Lydia was grinning at her. "He was charming man … Honey. Your father … a good man. Gregory Raymond Sinclair. I named you Ray after him."

"Oh, Mama!" She leaned over her mother and kissed her forehead as she stroked her hair.

"Didn't want you to know … because didn't want him to know."

"But, it would have helped me, I needed a father."

She seemed to gain some energy, "You haven't suffered. You're more perfect than any other girl I know. You didn't need to know him, Honey. You didn't need him. But now—" She turned away and coughed hard into the pillow.

Honey laid her hand on her mama's back and felt the wrenching gasps between the croaking coughs.

Finally Lydia turned back and looked up at her daughter with a drawn face and red-rimmed eyes. She said: "That diary ... is for you ... my dear. I won't be here ... much longer. Keep it with you. Read all of it. It's ... about the year before ... you were born." She coughed again, a painful cough, she winced. "He's your father ... we were in love ... didn't want to fall in love ... but ... did ... couldn't help it." She was struggling to breathe and was getting weaker. "Desire to have you ... stronger than love ... maybe did the wrong thing ... don't think so."

"It's alright, Mama. At least you've told me and that's enough," she lied. She thought of all the times how much easier it would have been to have had a father to talk to, to go to. Lydia was certainly a superwoman, but she was limited in her thinking. Honey had needed more than a mother.

Lydia seemed to gain another surge of strength and grasped Honey's arm. "I never contacted Gregory after I came home ... after those wonderful months ... on the south coast of England. I told him when we first met ... that I lived in New York and ... didn't tell him any different ... so he couldn't find me. Will you forgive me?" Her voice was strained and hoarse.

Honey could see the panic on her face. "Of course, Mama. It's alright now, don't worry. I'm just grateful you have at last told me the truth. I feel complete now. Do you understand what I mean? Now I feel normal, I have a father and I know who he is. He's real. It's a huge relief, actually."

"When you get home, Honey … the rest of my diaries are in my closet … in the blue trunk … the years of my life … now I'm getting tired … need to sleep … love you, dear … " Her voice trailed as she dropped into a deep slumber.

That night Honey's mama died.

That night Mama came to her in a dream: *standing beside Honey's bed, Lydia reached over and closed the lovely pink diary lying across her chest. She looked down at Honey with kind blue eyes and broad grin and whispered, "Don't read about your daddy; go find him."*

2

After her mother's memorial, Honey wasted no time; she put things in order and booked a direct flight on Virgin Airlines from Los Angeles to London. The eleven-hour non-stop flight would give her ample time to re-read more of mama's diary and prepare to meet her father, if he was still alive, if she could find him. She had to find him.

"Gregory and I have seen each other every day for two weeks. Only during lunchtime, though. We sit in front of the George Inn every day, sometimes having sandwiches, sometimes having fish and chips – his favorite. Fish and chips wrapped in newspaper, with vinegar sprinkled on the chips, and of course, beer. He loves his beer. He says his dream is to own a pub in Abbotsbury someday, which is a quaint little village just a short distance from Weymouth. He's going to take me there today. I think he might be the man I'm looking for to father my child. He seems to be

attracted to me. I certainly am attracted to him. We need to be having some night dates together, though. I don't know why he doesn't ask me out at night. I'm going to ask him today when he picks me up to go to Abbotsbury."

When Honey first read that passage her gut reaction told her he was a married man. When a man doesn't ask a woman out to dinner, only has lunch with her, he's usually married. They'd been seeing each other every day at lunchtime for two weeks? Definitely married. She stuck the diary in the pocket of the seat in front of her and unfastened the seat belt.

As she walked back to the toilet compartments, Honey couldn't help but notice loving couples sitting to the right and left on each side of the aisle. They were either sipping wine together - most likely on a holiday - leaning against each other or holding hands or kissing or whatever. It was a blatant reminder just how single she was, in her thirties without a man in her life and now, no immediate family whatsoever. Suddenly she was missing her mother desperately.

The few friends she had were either married or paired off. She was always the fifth wheel at any gathering, the odd man out. It was times like this when she traveled that it seemed to strike her the most. And it wasn't like she sat around pining away for some fairytale dreamboat to come into her life because she was usually too busy spending her time writing about romance rather than living it. Writing it seemed to take up the slack somewhat. *Romance is all around, but not for me,* kept running through her mind.

After returning to her seat, she decided to watch a movie and have a glass of champagne. She wasn't ready to read more about what happened next in the diary. As eager as she was to learn the story about her mother's love affair with her father, it was paining her. The memories and loss were hurting her. When the movie ended, she slept soundly for two hours and by the time she woke up the flight had been in the air five hours, only six more to go.

Staring at the diary in front of her in the seat pocket, she finally reached for it again.

"Hallelujah! We're going out to dinner tomorrow night. I asked him why he hadn't taken me out to dinner and he said he was afraid to. Said he couldn't trust himself with the moon and the sounds of the sea, it would be too romantic and more difficult for him to keep his hands off me. I smiled at the sincerity in his face, but doubted he was telling the truth, and told him not to worry, that we wouldn't do anything either of us didn't want to do. I was playing along. So he said he'd pick me up some night and we'd go to a pub for steak and ale near the docks. That was good enough for me.

"Abbotsbury was absolutely beautiful today. We went to the swannery and to the gardens. I see why he wants to live there. It's a quiet little village, but touristy. The tourists come to visit the swannery and the gardens by the busloads. It spite of the deluge, the village people and the tea rooms are inviting and lovely, it doesn't seem crowded. Everyone is polite and friendly.

"He said he'd like to take me to Dorchester next weekend; it's just a few miles from Weymouth too, more to

the east. That's where one of my favorite classic writers, Thomas Hardy, lived and wrote.

"I do hope Gregory's dream comes true and he gets his pub. There's only one in Abbotsbury. Right now he works on a fishing boat, though. Says they go out very early in the morning which is why he isn't out late at night. But he doesn't have to work this weekend and we have our first evening date tomorrow. Yippee! I like Gregory and I wouldn't mind living over here. But no, I can't be doing that. I came after my baby. That's all. I'm not here to find a man. Only a baby."

Well, so maybe he wasn't married. Maybe. Honey put the diary back in the mesh pocket, thinking how calculating it had to be to go on a search for a baby daddy with no intention to plan a life with the man. She never saw her mother as a woman who could be so manipulative. She felt a baby should have both parents to grow up well-rounded and feel loved in a proper way. But then again, Honey was well-rounded and never felt unloved, to the contrary, sometimes she felt smothered. She wondered what made the difference. She'd worked with children who were suffering from the single parent environment, children with serious emotional problems, most times abused children. That was it, there was the difference: abuse, neglect, lack of love and support.

"Excuse me, may I borrow the airline magazine, I didn't get one."

Honey leaned forward, retrieved it and handed it to the woman next to her. "There you go."

"Thank you. Are you from the States?" the older woman asked.

"Yes, I am. Going to Dorset for a holiday. You?"

"Going home after vacationing in California." She was chubby, about the age of Honey's mother.

"Where do you live in the UK?"

"In Bournemouth," the woman said.

"Oh, yes. That's not far from Weymouth, where I'll be staying."

"So you're off to Weymouth, are you?" the woman's interest piqued.

"Yes, I am."

Her face brightened. "You're taking the train from Heathrow?"

"Yes," Honey said.

"We'll be on the same train, then."

Honey wasn't sure if she wanted to strike up a friendship with and be talking to a chattering woman all the way to Bournemouth, so she did some quick thinking. "Well, actually, I'm staying in London for a few days before I go to Weymouth." She wasn't.

The woman slumped in disappointment. "Oh that's too bad; I could have used the company, it's such a long journey."

"I'm so sorry. Uh, will you excuse me?" Honey unbuckled her seatbelt and grabbed her purse, thinking she might stretch her legs a bit and at the same time avoid any further conversation.

Restless legs had kicked in as they usually did on long flights, poor circulation her doctor said. While she was walking up and down the aisle, she spied some empty seats back a few rows. So she returned to her seat, leaned in and grabbed her briefcase and the diary. The woman's eyes were closed as the music played in her ear phones, so she didn't even know that Honey had moved to another seat.

Something about airplanes, Honey preferred not to talk to passengers. Just not a friendly sort, she told herself, she either read or watched movies or slept. In a bar or a restaurant she would talk to anybody and everybody. The difference was because she could walk away or leave whenever she wanted. On a plane, she was stuck. But not this time, she was grateful the flight wasn't full.

Honey settled into the new seat, fastened her seatbelt and opened the diary to where she had left off.

"I'm waiting for Gregory, it's nearly seven forty-five. I've been ready since seven. This B & B is really comfy, I'm right on the seafront. I can hear the waves. The couple who owns it is such a delight and has made me feel at home. There's a Chinese restaurant across the road on the beach. I wonder if Gregory has been there. I think if this room were larger, I could live here easily. I wonder if Gregory has a house or lives in an apartment. I'm wearing a new gray outfit that I bought today at Marks & Spencer's - an ultra-conservative department store in the town mall. Quality clothing. It's one of the oldest department stores in England, opened in 1884 in Leeds. Fortnam and Mason in London is the oldest, 1707 ... Harrod's 1834. Oh, here he is! I'm so excited!"

It was time to rest her eyes; Honey felt a headache coming on. She slept for an hour until the sound of the food and beverage carts awakened her. Veggie lasagna and another glass of champagne were energizing. While eating she thought of her mama and wondered how she had kept the secret from her friends. Surely they must have known she was pregnant. How had she explained it when she began showing?

Her thoughts wandered to Weymouth. She planned to first go to the George Inn. Maybe someone there knew the whereabouts of Gregory Raymond Sinclair. She figured he would be retired by now, surely too old to be a fisherman. Or maybe sixty-year old fishermen didn't retire; age probably didn't matter in that line of work, although he said he wanted his own pub, according to the diary. Most likely he had married and had a family, if not before he met her mother, at least afterwards, it was so long ago. What could she say to him when she found him? She hadn't really thought about that. What if he didn't remember her mother? That would be a hardy blow. Now she was getting cold feet.

The hostess picked up the food tray and trash. Honey asked for coffee and reached for the diary, again.

"I am in love. I am! I don't want to go back to the states. Gregory wants me to stay here and marry him. Says he can't live without me. I don't know what to do. It's been two weeks since I've written in this diary. We have been together almost every day and night he's been home. He has a lovely house just outside of town on the road to Abbotsbury with a rose garden near the front gate and one of those lattice archways with the climbing roses. A lovely old farmhouse of gray stone; walls are at least two-feet

thick. His front door is painted red, a dark beet red. Gregory calls it royal red. The house belonged to his parents and he was an only child, he's never married. How can I do this? How can I stay here? If I marry him I can stay, I think. I can still be an American citizen and be married to a Brit. I can travel back and forth. Stay here six months at a time and make quick trips back to the U.S. to satisfy immigration. Or maybe I can get a permanent visa or dual citizenship. Oh, I don't know what to do.

"When we make love it is heaven, it is all I ever dreamed it would be. He does nothing wrong. I have never felt this way before. I didn't expect this. He is the most loving romantic man I've ever known, a fisherman in Dorset, who would've known. What a surprise!"

"Here's your coffee, Miss." The hostess handed a napkin and cup to Honey.

"Thank you so much." She set the diary aside and sipped the coffee while she thought back and remembered her mother's life. She couldn't help but feel sorry for her. All those years being there for Honey, all those years teaching school, all those years being where she didn't want to be when all she wanted was to be with her man in England. Why didn't she stay there or at least go back after Honey was born? Her mother had never loved anyone else. Honey had never seen her with a man, she never dated. When asked why she didn't date or get married, she said she wasn't interested. If she loved her fisherman in Dorset, why didn't she contact him? It was too much to take in. No wonder she had a headache.

3

Honey didn't pick up the diary again until she was on the train from London to Weymouth. The English countryside was something to behold, so green and velvety. It was raining, of course, living up to the rumor, and cold, around 45 degrees Fahrenheit. She was grateful she'd brought her favorite wool pea coat, wool scarves, hats and gloves. She was prepared.

This wasn't her first trip to England, she had been to London before, but hadn't traveled outside of the city. Such rich rolling green hills and rustic stone farmhouses dotted the landscape. Clusters of cottages nestled into the crevices between the hills forming the myriad of villages every few miles across the landscape. Each village had its own historic church with steeple rising above all else. The country roads were sprinkled with pedestrians dressed in their coats and boots, carrying umbrellas, walking their dogs. She knew England was a canine country, and regardless of the size of the animals, most lived indoors.

She'd been to France, Italy, Belgium and Switzerland, but never to the English countryside. So she enjoyed the train ride to Weymouth regardless of the weather. And most important of all, she'd upgraded to first class seating and hadn't run into the chubby woman from the plane, of that she was thankful.

"Something is wrong. Gregory was different last night. He hardly talked to me and didn't laugh at all. That's not like him. We've had such laughter bouts in the past few days. I'm worried. I'm feeling he's changed his mind, that he doesn't want to get married. I haven't said I would marry him, but I've hinted at the possibility. We've talked about me coming back at Christmas after I go home and make all the arrangements. My plane leaves for the U.S. tomorrow, school starts in two weeks. I have to leave for London today to make the connection tomorrow. I have been here for several months, and these last two wonderful months I'll never forget, regardless, no matter what happens. Gregory is taking me to the train station; he should be here any minute."

The station sign said 'Southampton.' Honey had to change trains. She tucked the diary under her arm, gathered up her belongings and hurried to the baggage rack near the exit. She'd learned how to travel light on other trips to Europe when doing research for her books, so she had one roller bag and a large shoulder bag, making maneuvering relatively easy. She attached the shoulder bag to the roller bag so the walk through airports and train stations was easier, taking the weight off her shoulder. If she could eliminate the shoulder bag, she would, but hadn't found a way to do that.

After stuffing the diary in the outside pocket of the roller bag, she was ready to exit the train. The last connection to Weymouth would be on another platform upstairs in ten minutes, so she had to hurry. That was cutting it pretty close, and she barely made it. She didn't read the diary on the final leg of the trip because the view from the train was so intriguing the rest of the way.

Sometimes pubs or inns rented out rooms above their restaurants, without listing them on the Internet, so she hadn't made advance room reservations in Weymouth; she wanted to check out the vicinity of the quay first, near the George Inn. Surely there were accommodations near the docks, she hoped.

A cabby drove her to the quay from the train station. There it was, the George Inn. Mama's George Inn. It was still there, probably looking the same as it did all those years ago when Mama was there. But there weren't any hotel rooms available. They did rent out rooms, they said, but they were all occupied.

Honey was directed to a large hotel up the promenade, back about a half mile towards the train station, but directly across from the beach. They also told her about a row of bed and breakfast hotels further up the Esplanade. She selected the stately Prince Regent Hotel. It was Victorian and elegant, had a restaurant and bar, looked appealing and very British. Perfect for now, she thought. She'd look at the B & B assortment the next day. All she wanted at that moment was a hot bath, a good dinner, and a nice long sleep in a comfy bed.

It was late by the time she unpacked, so she decided to grab a quick bite to eat and go to bed. She would set out on her quest the next day. Besides, the time change was eight hours ahead and it was a day later for her already. Leaving California at noon the day before and with only the few catnaps on the plane, she was exhausted. So by the time she bathed and freshened up before going downstairs for a meal, it was eight p.m. the next day already, and the time change was affecting her. She was dead on her feet, but hungry at the same time, feeling she needed something substantial other than plane and train food. Fresh grilled salmon and a huge green salad came to mind.

That night Honey slept twelve hours, didn't wake up till eleven the next morning. It was always hard for her to acclimate on trips to Europe from the U.S.; the return trip was much easier for some reason.

4

Honey woke up and took a quick shower, donned a pair of jeans and a pull-over sweater and took off towards the boat docks.

It was a lovely day, crisp, cool, just the kind of weather she loved.

Walking along the esplanade, which was a wide sidewalk bordering the pebbled and sand beaches with concrete flower boxes and benches, she could understand already why her mother had wanted to live there. It was beautiful. Unfortunate she hadn't returned.

Honey was carrying the diary in her shoulder bag, planning to read more during lunch. Of course she was going to the George Inn for a crab sandwich, just like her mama, all those years before.

The walk along the beachfront to the boat channel and the George Inn was stimulating. Yes, she already loved

Weymouth and she had been there only one night, didn't need any further convincing.

The research she'd done said the original George Inn was known to have existed on its same site since before 1665 when its owner, Sir Samuel Mico bequeathed it to the Corporation of Weymouth and Melcombe Regis - the settlement on the opposite bank of the channel. The profits from the Inn were to apprentice three poor children among other things and the charity continued to the present. She wondered before she came whether or not the George Inn would still be there, for in the states most businesses didn't last 20 years much less 220 years. So she was thrilled to have lunch on the very site her mother met her father.

Stepping through the Inn's door into a darkened pub, she smelled a mix of sea and mustiness, a waterfront ambiance. The aged wooden timbers and walls added to the quaintness. There were quite a few patrons scattered throughout the room, some at tables, others at the bar. All eyes turned on her as she entered, making her feel awkward and self-conscious.

She quickly sat on the first available barstool nearest the door. She'd found over the years that it was easy to learn more about the locals and the town by sitting at the bars instead of the tables. Conversation flowed easily, if not with the patrons sitting there, always with the barkeep.

"What would you like, darlin'?" the bartender asked.

"Do you serve wine?"

"Red or white?" he asked.

"White, please. Oh, wait. Do you have Champagne?"

"Yes, I do."

"By the glass?"

"Yes, we got that. Is that what you want, dearie?" He was a cheerful sort.

"That should do it. And one of your famous crab sandwiches, please."

"Would you like chips or salad with that, darlin'?"

"Salad, please, with vinaigrette," she said as she turned on the bar stool to take in the view of the entire room. She was sitting next to a partial wall, the entrance behind her, and could see down the length of the bar and the dining tables to the left of that section of the bar. There was a pool table situated in the center of the room.

Three rough-skinned, sunburned men, rugged types dressed in sweatshirts and jeans, were sitting at the opposite end of the bar. They were drinking beer and laughing loudly, all three with thick British accents, some words undecipherable to Honey's American ears. One man was older than the other two who were in their forties most likely. There were other groups of rugged men around the room, some at tables.

There was an adjoining room to her right on the other side of the partition and doorway. The L-shaped bar top and more stools continued to run the length of that room also, which had a more formal atmosphere of a fireplace and upholstered seating. The bartender serviced both rooms, two types of patronage. Honey imagined there would be at least two barkeeps when the place was busy on a Saturday night.

Men were sitting outside too, smoking and drinking, and there were a few women spaced here and there. Two came in and seated themselves between Honey and the three men further down the bar. Everybody seemed to know each other, friendly people.

She figured the George Inn had to be a locals' pub which was the best kind to frequent as a traveler. She did that wherever she went – find the local haunts, her first rule. But her mama was the reason for being in the George Inn.

"Here you go, your champagne, little lady. The sandwich is coming up. You from the States?"

"Yes, I am. Taking a holiday away from it all."

"I just got back from Florida, go there every year," he said.

"That's great. Have you ever been to California? That's where I live."

"No, but I am thinking about it. The owners went this year, after New Orleans. See the photo up there? That's them in New Orleans." He walked over to the three men and pulled more beer for them.

The photo drew Honey's attention to all the post cards and other photos that were tacked on the wall behind the bar. Post cards from travelers and friends, from far away places, and quite a few from the States.

She braved the question. "Do you happen to know Gregory Ray Sinclair? He was a fisherman around here thirty years ago."

The older man at the opposite end turned his head and looked at her. "You asking about our Greg Sinclair?"

"Yes, do you know him?"

"Haven't seen him in a few years. He retired from fishing. Doesn't come around here much anymore."

"Do you know if he's still in the area?" Honey was getting excited and was sure it was showing.

"So why you looking for him?" The man lifted his pint of beer and sipped, squinting at her over the top of the mug.

Everyone sitting at the bar including the bartender waited for her answer. She wasn't sure if she should divulge the real reason of her quest, didn't feel it was something they all should know. It was personal information only for her father's ears, if he was still alive she didn't want to embarrass him in front of his friends.

So, thinking quickly on her feet which was her forte, she said: "I—I'm a distant cousin, have only just found out that one branch of our family was from Dorset and I've traced some of them to Weymouth. You know us Americans; we love to claim our British heritage. I'm just hoping I can find him or any of his family still living in the area."

Another man from one of the tables stepped up to the bar, "As a matter of fact, I was his brother-in-law."

"Was? You mean he's dead?" Her heart stopped as fear engulfed her.

"No, it was me sister. His wife. She died ten years ago. I haven't seen him for years, but then he wasn't much of a socializer with our family. After me sister died we didn't hear much from him."

"Are there any children?" She restrained herself.

"No. They had one way back, but it was stillborn. They didn't try for any more after that."

No children, he was still alive a few years ago. She took a deep breath and then took a sip of her drink, mind whirring, as she tried to organize her thoughts.

One of the young men sitting at the bar added, "I saw him a couple weeks ago at the Cove. You know, on Chesil Beach? He'd been out fishing with his mates, they were having Sunday lunch. I overheard him say he was glad to have a day off from working his pub in Abbotsbury."

"Didn't know he had a pub in Abbotsbury," the older man said.

"I was with me in-laws, so didn't go over and talk to him. We were getting ready to leave."

Honey was soaking it all up and getting more excited by the moment, and was getting hotter by the minute, could feel her face flushing, and her heart beating wildly. She needed a breather.

The bartender brought the crab sandwich to her.

"Do you mind if I take my lunch outside and watch the boats?" she asked. She needed to get out of there to compose herself.

"Not at all, here let me help you carry it." He came around the bar and carried her food and drink outdoors.

"Thank you so much. I'll bring the plate and glass back in when I finish."

"No problem, take your time." He went back into the pub.

She could see the patrons at the bar through the open door and could hear the laughter and the conversation that would switch back and forth between loud and a constant hum.

The sandwich was still as good as her mama had said it was. With closed eyes she tried to visualize the day her father met her mother, probably in that very spot where she was sitting.

"Excuse me, Miss. The birds are eating your food."

Honey opened her eyes to see a man lifting her plate and shooing birds away.

"If it's your plan to feed them your sandwich, then that's all right, but I don't think that is the plan, am I right?" He set the plate back down on the bench beside her and sat on the other side of it. Then he stretched his arms out across the back of the bench, staring at Honey and grinning widely.

She was speechless, still staring at him.

"Are you all right? I didn't mean to startle you," he said, looking at her with dark piercing eyes.

"Uh, yes. I'm okay. I mean, well, I was just somewhere else, that's all. Sorry. Thank you. I didn't see the birds."

"They love crab meat. You're eating their favorite meal, you know."

"Oh, I didn't know that. I didn't know." She couldn't believe she was looking into the face of the most rugged, handsome man she'd ever seen. He was dark brown from the sun; at least it appeared to be a suntan. Either from working outdoors, or maybe he was a sailor, a fisherman. Her mind ran wild with assumptions. He didn't appear to be of a darker race, but he could be. His accent was British.

"So, are you American?" he asked.

"Yes, I am. You?"

"French, have lived in Paris most of my adult life. I was born in Saint Malo, straight across the channel from here. My father operated his fishing boat in the channel since before I was born. Actually, I'm French and Portuguese, my mother is from Portugal, her father was a fisherman. I'm from a long line of fisherman."

"Oh, then you might know my cousin, Greg Sinclair. He was a fisherman here in Weymouth."

"My father might. My parents live here now, Dad is retired. They live at the east end of the promenade between Greenhill and Preston. I'm normally in Paris, only come here to visit. I'll ask him. Greg Sinclair?"

"Yes, thank you. One of the guys in the pub thinks he runs a pub in Abbotsbury."

"Have you been to Abbotsbury?" his eyes brightened.

"No, I haven't. My name is Honey, by the way, what's yours?"

"Honey?" He laughed. "Are you kidding me?"

"No, I'm not kidding you. That's what my mother named me. You can imagine all the teasing I've been subjected to and worse yet, my full name is Honey Ray Howard. HRH. The kids teased me all through school."

The man displayed the widest grin and the whitest teeth she'd ever seen. "I am Jean Vincent Doucet. People call me Jean Vincent as if it's one word. And I will not make fun of your name. It is a beautiful name and eliminates the difficulty of remembering. I would imagine your husband finds it very easy—"

"I'm not married, but yes, the boyfriends, few that there were, found it easy to remember."

Honey took a bite of her sandwich as Jean Vincent drank his beer. She could feel his eyes on her as she pretended to watch a fishing boat maneuver broadside to the pilings.

Finally Jean Vincent broke the silence and stood, "Would you like me to take you to Abbotsbury after you have your lunch? My car is near."

She looked up at him, "Well, I don't know—"

"Everyone in the pub will vouch for me, they all know me. I would be happy to do this for you."

He was such a handsome figure standing there warming her all over with his penetrating gaze. She was feeling helpless all of a sudden, feeling feminine for the first time in years, feeling all tingly and giddy. It was ridiculous, she thought, she was acting like a schoolgirl. She had to get control of herself.

Finally, "No, that's all right. Thank you, but I've some other things I must do before I go to Abbotsbury. Thank you. You're most gracious."

She thought she saw disappointment on his face, but felt it would be frivolous and ridiculous for her to accept a stranger's offer to cart her around the countryside. He could be a serial killer, a rapist, for all she knew. It would be foolish for her to accept his offer. No. She couldn't do that.

"If you change your mind, I'll be back here around six this evening. That should give you time to take care of your errands. And it will take just a few minutes to get to the pub in Abbotsbury, so we can have a meal there, if you wish."

Why am I hesitating? Say no! It would be madness to take off with a stranger, especially at night.

"Let me do that for you, show you some local courtesy."

"Okay. Yes. I'll be back at six. Thank you." *I must be crazy.*

"Then I will be off to take care of a few errands myself. Honey, it's been a pleasure talking to you and I'll see you at six tonight?"

"Yes, at six." She couldn't believe she agreed to let him take her. *Pure craziness!*

5

It was five o'clock later that afternoon and Honey took one last look at herself in the mirror. She wished she were shorter. Her tall lanky body didn't fit her vision of an attractive woman. Silver strands of hair were beginning to appear around her face, but it wasn't bad. The rest of her thick black hair made up for it. Actually her hair was quite beautiful; it was wavy and shoulder length. She always thought it was her saving grace. She groomed herself quite well: skin, nails, the way she carried herself, perfection. But she felt her nose was too big and her mouth too small. She wished they'd been reversed. Plastic surgery had been a possibility, but she never took the time for it when it might have mattered. She hadn't thought about it in years, till now.

She grabbed her pea coat and bag and set off at a rapid clip along the boardwalk, heading towards town and the George Inn to meet a tall, dark, handsome man. Her plan was to get there before him and have a glass of wine to relax a bit. She was nervous.

Earlier in the afternoon after lunch before returning to the hotel, she walked to the mouth of the harbor and watched passengers disembark the gigantic hovercraft that had just arrived from Saint Malo. The ferries made the trip across the English Channel several times a day, between Weymouth and France. Looked like something she'd like to do.

She made a mental note to do an Internet search on Saint Malo, to see what kind of seaport it was and learn more about the birthplace of Jean Vincent. Thoughts of him crept into her mind at every turn, in every shop she browsed. She even thought of him while dressing for the date, if a date was what it was, she wasn't sure. She wondered if he would like this or that sweater, this or that pair of pants, and this or that pair of boots. Settling on all black was pretty simple since wearing black was her norm.

It was a cool early evening, nippy, but not freezing. The sea breeze against her face felt good. She loved the smell of the crisp ocean air in Weymouth. It was a clean and natural town, no foul smells, no garbage littering the streets as it was in New York City the last time she'd been there. As exciting as NYC was, the smells were horrific. She figured one gets used to it when living in it, but she had difficulty not covering her nose and mouth to prevent breathing in the awful stench.

Weymouth smelled good. Even as she reached the bridge that crossed the harbor channel, the docks smelled of fresh sea air and fish, not stale fish, it was an inviting aroma. Steep stone steps led down from the bridge to the quayside where she breathed in more invigorating air.

Inside the George Inn she sat at the bar on the same stool she'd occupied earlier. The bartender was preparing to leave, a shift change. He recognized her and gave her a cheerful greeting. She ordered a white Zinfandel, relaxed, and took in more of the local color.

A hand touched her shoulder and she turned to face Jean Vincent. He didn't look like the same man she'd met earlier that day. His black hair was slicked back which made his dark eyes even more dominant and sparkly, his clean-shaven face softened his tanned skin, and his attire was entirely unexpected – a black leather flight jacket and a gray turtle-necked cashmere sweater with matching wool flannel slacks, black Italian loafers shined to perfection. She was taken aback.

He misinterpreted her surprise. "Oh? You expect someone else?"

"No, no," Honey laughed. "I just didn't expect you to look like you do. You were a bit more rugged before."

"That was my daytime look; this is my nighttime look. You like?" he said as he twirled around. There was that inviting grin again.

"Oh yes, I like. You're very handsome. I suppose everyone tells you that, though, so I take it back."

He laughed heartily. "So I shouldn't tell you how beautiful you are, because everyone tells you, yes?"

"As a matter of fact, only my mother told me that. So you're quite safe, it won't go to my head. Thank you."

"And is your mother waiting for you back in the States?"

The question startled her. "Well, no. She died two weeks ago." Honey fought back a wave of tears, always lurking, ready to fall at thoughts of her mother.

"I'm so sorry. I didn't mean to be flippant, I didn't know."

"It's okay. Really. She was sick for quite some time. She's peaceful now. It's okay. I'm coming to terms with it." She wiped her eyes with her fingers.

"I'll have a pint, John," he called out to the bartender. "Do you mind if I have a drink before we go?"

"Of course not. In fact I think I'll have another."

"Bring another for the lady, John, while you're at it." He sat on the stool next to her. "Why are you looking for Sinclair? To tell him about your mother?"

"Yes, but mainly because I want to meet him and my other British relatives, of course."

"I made a few calls this afternoon to see if he is in Abbotsbury, and was told he does own a pub there, but couldn't find out anything more about him. So I know where it's located."

Goose bumps popped up on her arms and her hair felt as if it were standing straight up. *I am so close to meeting my father. What if he rejects me? What if he says 'so what?'*

"Are you all right?" Jean put his hand on Honey's arm where she had pushed up her sleeve. "You are cold?"

"No, I'm fine, I'm fine, really."

6

It was picture perfect driving into Abbotsbury along the main street that was lined with thatched roofed cottages, just as Honey's mama had written in her diary, and it was truly beautiful, even at night. The cozy lamps shone through the cottage windows and gave off a luminescent, inviting feeling. It felt as if it would be alright to walk up to any door and no doubt be welcomed by friendly inhabitants – strangers or not.

What a lovely village! No wonder mama loved this place. "This is beautiful, Jean Vincent!" Her neck felt strained looking back and forth from one side of the street to the other. "Just like mama said."

"Your mother was here?"

"Yes, she was." She didn't mean to let that slip. "Years ago."

"Some of these thatched stone cottages date back to

the sixteenth century. The streets meet and broaden in the square up ahead near the pub and the bus stop. The Ilchester Arms, Greg Sinclair runs, is one of the pubs, or public houses as they used to call them. There it is, up ahead. See that opening between the buildings to the left of it? That was used for the horse-drawn coaches to pull through and stop at the inside entrance to unload and pick up passengers. I'll park the car out here on the street; it appears this is as close as we're going to get. Looks busy tonight."

Suddenly Honey was frightened. She recalled the portion of Mama's diary she had read that afternoon.

"I was dumbfounded when Gregory told me at the train station he was getting married in two months, that it had been planned long before he knew me and that it wouldn't be appropriate for me to come back at Christmas. He had tears in his eyes when he said he loved me and that he meant it when he asked me to marry him. But the families had always expected him to marry Louise Becker.

"He and Louise had grown up together and had always been an item. She'd been in the States for the past two years at university and had suddenly returned the day before, unannounced. He said he was sad and heartbroken, said he'd hoped Louise wouldn't come back at all and had been trying to figure out how to tell her and her family about me.

"He held me and said he would always love me, he just couldn't tell Louise. He was fond of her, he said, and didn't want to hurt her. He said he would never love her as he did me, and that he felt confused, but if I'd please stay in

contact with him he'd try to find a way that we could be together.

"I felt as if a knife had stabbed me in the heart and its serrated edges were twisting and turning, ripping at me. I felt as if an iron-clad fist had plunged into my belly and struck my back bone. I felt as if a rope had tightened around my throat and was squeezing the life out of me. I couldn't breathe, I couldn't think, I couldn't bear the thought of living without him. I reached into my pocket and squeezed a piece of paper into a tight wad. I had written my real address and phone number on the piece of paper to give to him before I left. The tears blurred my vision as I turned and ran to board the train without looking back. I never looked back. I never saw or spoke to him again."

Honey shook her head and wondered what might have happened if mama had given him the piece of paper with her real address and phone number. She couldn't imagine anyone rejecting her mother and she felt she should have tried to work out something with him. Of course her mama didn't know she was pregnant yet. Honey couldn't imagine how her mama managed to overcome her broken heart and raise a daughter as well as she did, all the while seeing her child's father in her, every single minute of every single day. Maybe that was how she coped, knowing she had a part of him with her. Honey could only guess.

Now Honey was going to meet him. What if he didn't care to know her? What if he felt she was an intruder in his life? Someone who didn't belong. The negative thoughts were running rampant. She'd read and heard about other adult children being rejected by a birth parent. Why should she even think he might want her in his life? Her mother had totally excluded him as if he never existed. How would he feel about that? He didn't even know he had a daughter. How could she expect him to love and accept her? She was terrified as she walked through the doorway.

The pub was a charming one, homey and friendly, very British, although not as rustic and dark as the George Inn in Weymouth. The patrons in the Abbotsbury pub were mostly locals with a few tourists that were staying in nearby accommodations.

Behind the bar was a tall, strapping man, ruddy complexioned, happy eyes and countenance, black hair, a crop of silver at his temples. He looked more Italian than English. Beside him was a younger woman, although older than Honey, serving up drinks at one end of the bar, and there was a cook in the kitchen and a food server. Only four people manned the busy establishment.

Of course in England it was much easier to serve the public in pubs, especially smaller ones like this one. No waiters or waitresses, it was self-order from a huge chalk board on the wall giving the meals of the day, and self-serve.

The laughter and loud voices made it even more hospitable and fun loving. Honey felt comfortable, especially with Jean Vincent's arm around her as they stood inside the door taking it all in.

"Shall we find a place at the bar?" Jean Vincent asked as he took a step in that direction.

Honey couldn't take her eyes off the man behind the bar. "Sure. I prefer sitting at the bar. I'd rather eat there, too, if you don't mind."

"That's exactly what I had in mind."

They found two seats at the far end. It was the perfect spot to watch who Honey thought might be her father working that end of the bar.

"Good evening to you both and what would you like to drink on this festive occasion?" the man asked as he approached them, grinning from ear to ear.

"The lady will have a White Zinfandel and I'll have a pint of the dark, thank you."

"All right. Comin' right up!" He walked away.

Honey couldn't help but feel a connection to the man; *he's got to be my father*. They had the same color hair and eyes. Her nose was his. She was tall like him. Left-handed like him. Both had clefts in their chins. She wondered if maybe he was Greek. Greek – Italian, maybe?

"Here you go," the barman said when he returned with their drinks. "Are you going to be dining with us tonight?"

"Yes, we are," Honey responded. "What do you suggest?"

"Roast Lamb for the gentleman, yes? And we've a delicious poached salmon for the lady, both served with steamed vegetables and potatoes."

"Sounds yummy to me. What do you think, Jean Vincent?"

"We'll have exactly what you suggest, but let's wait a while, shall we? Say in about thirty minutes or so before you put in the order? And we'll dine right here, if we may."

"Of course. Enjoy your drinks and relax right where you are. Are you from around here, lassie?" He was looking curiously at Honey, staring actually.

"No, I'm not. I'm from America. I've come here to visit my relatives."

"What is your family name, maybe I know them." His eyes were searching Honey's face as if she reminded him of someone.

"She thinks you might be related to her, as a matter of fact. You're Gregory Sinclair aren't you?" Jean Vincent startled Honey with his abruptness.

"That I am, yes, Greg Sinclair. And who might you be, young lady? I didn't know I had any relatives in the U.S."

"My … my mother was Lydia Howard. Do you remember her?" Her heart was beating out of her chest, tears were coming to her eyes. She could feel the flush rise to her cheeks and spread in every direction.

Sinclair gasped as he moved his hands from the bar and put them on his hips, stepped back and took in a deep breath. He stared directly at Honey for a few moments then turned in a circle, running his hands through his hair. When he looked at her again he had tears in his eyes too.

"I—I'm your daughter. My name is Honey Ray Howard. She named me after you, my middle name."

Gregory was flabbergasted and was finding it difficult to speak, emotions overtaking him. He pulled a handkerchief from his pocket and wiped his eyes, looked as if he was going to cry out loud.

"Are you all right? I didn't mean to be so abrupt, but I've been so eager to find you. Too much time has been wasted and I just had to jump in feet first. I'm sorry; I hope you're all right," she was on the verge of crying.

"Oh yes, yes. I'm perfectly all right. I just never dreamed— how is she? How is Lydia? Did she come with you?" He looked over the heads of the customers toward the door.

"No. She passed away two weeks ago." Tears were ready to fall.

"Oh no! Not my Lydia!" He buried his face into his handkerchief and wept, turning towards the wall trying to control his crying.

"I'm so sorry," Honey said, stretching her hand towards him, wiping her eyes with the other hand. "I didn't know about you till just before she died when she finally told me. She wanted me to come find you. She said I looked like you and I think that made her feel close to you all those years. She never married, raised me alone. She was a wonderful, loving mother."

Jean Vincent took it all in, hadn't said a word since Honey began talking. He tightened a supportive grip on Honey's shoulder as she continued in almost a whisper.

"I don't want anything from you, Papa; I just want to have a chance to get to know you. I've not had a father all my life. And well, I guess it's better late than never. You know?" Now the tears were running down her cheeks.

Gregory blew his nose and looked her over once again. "You're right about that, Lassie." He quickly lifted the bar gate and went straight towards her. "Let me hug my

46

little girl, Laddie. This is my baby girl."

Sinclair lifted his daughter off the bar stool and held her so tight she gasped.

It felt better than any hug she'd ever had. She couldn't believe her real father was holding her at last. She couldn't stop the tears that had been stored inside her since she was a little girl and first asked her mama who her daddy was and then through all the years of wondering.

"My daughter, everybody! I have a girl I didn't know I had!" He stood beside Honey and held up her hand in his, as if he was declaring a winner to the audience. "She's come to meet me! Here she is! This is my little Honey Ray!"

7

Two weeks later Honey wrote on the page after her mama's last entry in her Christmas diary.

"Mama, I have met my papa. He is everything you said he was. He said he never got over losing you and his childless marriage was an unhappy one. He really loved you, Mama. And I understand why you loved him and wanted to live here.

"Dorset is absolutely beautiful. And Mama, you aren't going to believe this, I met a lovely man in the very same spot you met Papa. I was eating a crab sandwich just like you when Jean Vincent came out of the George Inn and sat by me. I've never met a man as charming and kind. Except for Papa.

"I'm meeting daddy in the morning and I think I'm going to stay for awhile to get to know him and maybe help him out in his pub, if he'll let me. Yes, he bought his pub in

Abbotsbury several years ago and has beautiful living quarters upstairs, nine rooms. You would love it, Mama. I know you would.

"Mama, my papa is of Italian heritage. Irish – Italian. His mama was Irish, he was born here.

"I love you and I miss you so much."

Honey packed her bags and rented a car for the drive to Abbotsbury. She spent almost every day of the two weeks from the first night in Abbotsbury with her papa. He had insisted she check out of the hotel and move upstairs at the pub, said there was plenty of room; she'd have own bedroom, sitting room and bath.

The upstairs quarters were set up to be nine ensuite tourist accommodations, but Sinclair used two of them as his own living space. He said once in a while he would rent out all the rooms, if it was necessary, to a patron who couldn't make it home after a night of heavy drinking, but usually no. When he did that, he would drive home to Weymouth where his own cottage was, the family home, belonged to his parents when they were alive.

As Honey drove the short distance through the hilly countryside from Weymouth to Abbotsbury, excited about moving in with her father, she remembered her life as it used to be and how it might be if she were to stay in England. She imagined how her mother must have gone through the same mental and emotional process when she was faced with the decision.

Rounding the last corner entering Abbotsbury, she saw a commotion outside her papa's pub. People were standing around; some were going in and out of the pub in a frantic-like manner. Luckily there was a parking space opposite on the square and she grabbed it before anyone else could. There was a line of cars behind her.

Honey left the luggage in the car. Since she didn't recognize anyone, she went through the door and spotted the barmaid. "Hannah, what's going on?"

"Oh, Missy. Your father's been taken to hospital in Weymouth. A heart attack. They just pulled off no more than ten minutes ago."

"Where is the hospital?" Honey screamed.

She drove as fast as she could and still be able to control the car on the narrow two-lane road. The hospital was easy to find with Hannah's directions. Her papa had been there thirty minutes by the time she was ushered to the area where they were working on him. She was crying before she saw him, and cried even harder when she did see him.

His eyes were closed, he was ashen. Tubes were running all over the place, monitors beeping. He was hooked up to a ventilator ... it was an uncanny replay of her mother. This couldn't be happening again. Honey was devastated.

She caressed her papa's big, rough hand, squeezed it, kissed it, and laid her hand on his brow, talking to him. "Papa, please don't go. Please don't leave me now. I just found you. You can't leave me. I need you."

He opened his eyes and looked directly at his loving daughter and squeezed her hand. He couldn't talk because of the tube down his throat, but his eyes told her that he loved her and didn't want to go.

"I love you too, Papa. Mama loved you very much, and I love you too."

The corners of his mouth formed a smile and he took his last breath.

"Mama, I'm sure you already know this; Papa died three days ago, the service was today. I was there when he took his last breath, Mama. I told him you loved him, and I hope that he has found you by now. I've put aside my grief and am replacing it with the romantic notion that he just couldn't bear to live without you any longer, he's in search of you, Mama. He left this world four weeks to the day you left.

"The day before his heart attack, he drew up a will with his solicitor leaving me the business in Abbotsbury and the house outside Weymouth. He still had that house, Mama, the one with the royal red door.

"I feel like I'm home in Abbotsbury. I feel like this is where I should have been born, with you and papa here in Dorset. I'm staying, Mama. I can write anywhere, so it doesn't matter where I live, we both know that.

"And Jean Vincent is comforting to me. We've become even closer through all this. We've been intimate, and I'm feeling as if it's a replay of how it was for you

when you were here with Papa. The only difference this time, however, is that I'm going to stay – for you and for me."

PART TWO

Honey's Diary

Rebecca Buckley

8

Dear Diary:

"Today has been a difficult day for me. It's raining and the sky is black. Gloomy. I've been thinking of Mama and Papa a lot. Jean Vincent is returning from France tonight, so I'll be happy to see him. He's been away for three weeks and I really have missed him.

"I still don't know what kind of work he does, he says he does as little as possible when I ask that question, and then he laughs and changes the subject. I feel uneasy when he does that, just can't seem to pin him down. In fact, lately he is distant and I feel he would rather be somewhere else than with me. Could be my paranoia setting in, but it sure seems as if there's been a shift in our relationship.

"It's probably my imagination, my own insecurities; heaven knows I've got plenty of those. I mean it isn't as if my track record with men has been a stable

one. It's been years since I've had a relationship. And when I met Jean Vincent, I was like a fly to honey. I am the metal to his magnet. No choice in the matter whatsoever. I'm drawn. I'm sunk. I know that must have been how Mama felt when she met Papa.

"Oh well, I'm not going to think about it right now. Time to go to work."

As Honey drove to Abbotsbury the rain clouds moved away and the sun sent its rays to dry the green pastures and trees. A good day to go to Abbotsbury Gardens, she was thinking. Maybe take Hannah there for lunch after the pub lunch crowd dissipated. The new girl, Lottie, could handle it by herself. Yes, that's what she would do.

She rolled down the car window as she drove and breathed in the fresh aroma, feeling the cool breeze on her face. Nothing smelled better than the elements after a good rain, and everything glistened as the sun reflected from the abundance of emerald leaves and grass.

There was more traffic than usual on the two-lane country road to Abbotsbury. It didn't mean everybody was going to the village, though. Bridport, a popular seaside port, was beyond Abbotsbury, and some travelers would cut over from the Abbotsbury road and head east to Dorchester too. But still the village got its fair share of holiday spenders on their way to the swannery and the gardens. And most would want a cold beer to soothe their tiring body after traipsing through both tourist attractions.

Luckily the pub was situated halfway between the gardens and swannery on the road that ran through the middle of the village between the two sites. So business was thriving.

"There she is," Hannah called out to Honey as she came through the front door.

The pub was full, the bar and the tables. Honey was thankful she had hired two new people, an additional one for the kitchen and another bar person. It was one of those days that proved she did the right thing. This was all new to her, being in the hospitality business. She still wasn't sure of what she was doing most of the time, but in this instance she had called it right.

"Nice crowd," she said as she grinned at Hannah while quickly putting her bag away and seeing to the requests of the patrons.

On busy days like this she would walk around the room making sure the diners had everything they needed, drinks, condiments, extra napkins, conversation, and she'd clear the tables before seating other customers. During the dinner hour, a busboy was on duty, but lunch usually didn't warrant it. The lunch crowd was too uncertain and sporadic, but Honey was on call if it got too busy to handle. It worked out great, because she lived only fifteen minutes away. Honey's regular hours were from three in the afternoon till closing. So she did have a regular shift to do the books and manage the staff.

It appeared she was settling in quite nicely, her new lifestyle seemed to fit and she was happy.

* * * * *

Lunch at the Abbotsbury Gardens was peaceful. Honey loved going there and did it quite often to feed the birds and listen to the sounds of nature while lunching on the veranda.

"Will Jean Vincent be returning soon?" Irish Hannah asked as she pushed her plate away and began sipping coffee.

"Today, actually. Tonight. I don't know if he'll come to the pub, he may just meet me at home. I'll know later." Honey wondered about his new routine. He would call and arrange to meet at home instead of the pub. He used to come to the pub. She'd meant to ask him about it, but hadn't yet.

"How is it going with him, if you don't mind me asking you?"

"In what way?" Honey looked at her inquisitive employee.

"Well, I mean, is it serious? Are you in love with him?"

"I don't know how to answer that. Serious? In a way I suppose it is. With me anyway. I'm not sure how he feels."

"I don't mean to pry at you; I just remembered something your father said to me one day."

"What was that?"

Hannah, shifted in her chair, sat up straight and poured more coffee from the carafe. "Well, he said, 'Hannah, I'm not so sure about this fella that's a courtin' my sweet daughter.' Called him fella, he did." She laughed. "He said he wasn't sure if he was the right one for you. Said he was worrisome. Seemed mysterious. Did he not say that to you?"

"No, he didn't. We didn't talk much about Jean Vincent. It was all about my papa and me."

"And it was a good thing, wasn't it?" Hannah's eyes began to water. "I really miss him, I do."

Honey reached across the table and touched her hand. "I know you do. You were very close to him, I know."

"If I had been just a little bit older I think he would have looked at me differently. I had such a crush on him. But he treated me like a younger sister." She laughed. "A kid, can you imagine? A forty-five year old kid."

"Oh Hannah, I didn't know, I mean— but I remember that night we first came into the pub, I did think you might be his girlfriend. Why didn't you pursue him?"

"No no no. I couldn't do that. He was my boss. That would've been the death of me. He didn't look at me that way. No no no." She laughed harder.

"Well, I'm so happy you were there for him. He talked about how valuable you were, said you were his best employee. And I'm glad you stayed on." Honey took a sip of coffee. "I don't know what he meant about Jean Vincent being mysterious and worrisome, though. That was a strange thing to say, wasn't it?" But she was beginning to agree with her papa's observation.

9

Jean Vincent telephoned Honey later that night just as she figured he would. She told him she'd be home around ten-thirty.

As much as she wanted to see him for it had been a while, she was feeling weary and wishing she could just go home and go to bed. It had been a long day. A long busy day. It seemed she was more tired than usual lately.

Her doorbell rang at eleven.

When she opened the door, Jean Vincent was holding a bouquet of white daisies, a bottle of wine, and grinning, exuding appeal, and was as handsome as ever. Honey's heart melted. The tiredness disappeared.

"Come in, come in. Here let me take those, I'll put the flowers in water."

"How about a kiss first," he said and leaned towards her. He put his arms around her, holding the daisies and wine behind her back. The slight kiss became a romantic kiss, then a thrilling kiss, the type that could go on and on increasing in pleasure if the two allowed it.

Honey pulled back first. "Now that was some kiss! Wow! I need to catch my breath. Give me those flowers and that bottle of wine, will you?"

He handed them to her and she went off to the kitchen. He removed his leather jacket and hung it over the back of a chair, then sat on the sofa, waiting.

Soft music was playing and candles were flickering, there was a slight aroma of Champaka incense in the air. He loved the way Honey would set the scene for his arrival. It made him feel special. What he didn't know was that she did it for herself every evening; it was soothing to her, relaxing. She'd done it for years.

Every night she would create a calm, pleasant atmosphere and pour a glass of wine to sip while she relaxed either in a bath or in an overstuffed chair, listening to music or reading.

"Here we are, a glass for you, and one for me. How was your trip?" She sat next to him on the sofa.

"It was ... the usual. Nothing to speak of." He lifted his glass to hers. "A toast, shall we? To this evening, to us." They both sipped.

"How was it in Paris?" She tried once again to get him to talk about his life.

"It was hectic. I met with old friends who want me to go into a business venture with them."

"Oh? What kind of business?"

"It's nothing. Nothing. Let's talk about you. I want to hold you, Honey. It's been too long." He gulped the rest of his wine, then took her glass and set both their glasses on the cocktail table. "I've been dreaming about this." He drew her to him and smothered her face with gentle kisses. He lifted her hands and kissed them to the tips of her fingers, then he nestled his soft lips under her chin and followed the hollow down to her breasts.

His fingers were unbuttoning her caftan just ahead of his kisses and he cupped her breasts with his hands and kissed their tips, taking Honey's breath away.

Before she knew it, he lifted her and carried her to the bedroom, his mouth on hers as they went. Conversation was over before it began, as usual.

Honey couldn't resist him, ever, she melted under his touch.

"Darling, I have missed you so much," he whispered as he pushed her caftan aside and drew a nipple into his mouth, first one and then the other.

Her moans let him know how much she loved what he was doing and it drove him on even further. He replaced his mouth with his fingers, teasing, squeezing, tugging, and watching her face as the thrill increased for both of them.

She opened her eyes and breathlessly whispered, "I want you."

"Not yet," he said. He ran his tongue down her belly and below, finding her most sensual sex organ, titillating it with his tongue; sending her near to the edge of oblivion.

Heavenly oblivion, she called it.

Then he rose up and began kissing her mouth again, while with one hand adeptly opened his pants.

She gasped and sighed when he eased into her effortlessly in a rhythmic motion, in and out, in and out. He caused her to rise and fall with him, both endeavoring to reach the pinnacle of their desires.

The only sounds over the next hour were those made by the two of them, sounds of excitement and thrill, heightened sounds of sensual, sexual satisfaction.

And that was the way it was every time they were together.

10

Dear Diary:

"I don't know what happened. A month ago I got a phone call from Jean Vincent, calling from Saint Malo where he'd been for two weeks, he said. He also said he would be going to Paris, didn't know exactly for how long, but would let me know as soon as he found out.

"I've waited and waited for him to contact me. That was a month and a half ago. I expected him to call and tell me where he is and why, and to say he misses me and can't wait to get back. But he hasn't done that. I just can't believe he could go away without some sort of explanation. It isn't like we're casual friends. I know we haven't been seeing each other very long, but we've spent some very intimate times together. Sometimes he stays overnight, sometimes a full weekend. I am confused.

"I've tossed and turned, wondering if it's something

I've done, or didn't do, said or didn't say. I tried to reach him again this morning, but only got his message machine with its damn generic greeting."

She set her diary on the wrought iron table beside her and stood near the railing on the front porch of her papa's house, now hers. The busy traffic passing by was going south to Weymouth or in the opposite direction towards Abbotsbury, some eastward to Thomas Hardy country - Dorchester.

Her thoughts were of Jean Vincent. She just didn't get it. Questions flooded her mind. Why couldn't he tell her why he had to leave and for how long? Did he really have to go, or was he just putting her off, escaping? Maybe he had a wife and family in Paris. She had a queasy, uneasy feeling in her stomach. It was upsetting. She'd never been in a relationship with the magnitude of feelings she had for Jean Vincent. She wondered if her father felt that way when her mother left him those many years ago, disappearing, never to contact him again, leaving him to wonder in his heartbreak.

Her cell phone rang. She grabbed it from the table hoping it was Jean Vincent. It was Hannah, at the pub.

"Yes, Hannah?"

"Darlin', we've got a problem here. All the sinks are plugged up, won't drain," she said.

"Do we have a regular plumber?"

"Yes we do, shall I call him?"

"Of course. Right away. And I'll be there as soon as I can. Go ahead and call him, okay?"

"I will. Goodbye."

Hannah was priceless. Honey knew very little about the pub business, knew nothing about business in general, period, especially business in Britain. Knew nothing about the taxes or laws, absolutely nothing.

If her father would have lived he could have taught her, he probably would have. But that wasn't a choice now. She needed to do some quick, heavy-duty, learning. It had been four months since his heart attack, and she just didn't have time to do any more grieving over anybody. Nobody. She felt anger towards her papa, Jean Vincent, even her mama at that very moment for leaving her in such a lurch.

She wondered what lesson God was trying to teach her. How to lose everybody you love and survive it? How to feel absolutely alone in the world? Well, if that was the case, He had succeeded on the last count, but she was failing on the first.

Actually, she reminded herself, she had Hannah. She had her editor back in the States and her agent. In spite of it all, they were depending on her to pull herself together. She wouldn't give up. She hadn't been writing, but would get back to it as soon as the pub was working on its own. That was the plan anyway.

The thought came to her in a flash ... *I'll hire a general manager, someone who knows the business.*

She grabbed her purse and headed for the car.

11

The first time she got sick was after meeting Derrick Collins. Derrick had managed pubs and hotels all over Britain, mostly London. He had just moved to Weymouth from London after quitting his job there. Hannah knew him through some of her London friends and told him about the pub in Abbotsbury and what was needed; she arranged the meeting for that Monday morning.

He brought his CV and several letters of recommendation which were top notch. Honey told him she'd check out everything and would let him know by Friday.

The deal was that he would manage the entire food and beverage operation and the rooms upstairs. Honey had decided to rent out all the rooms. Hannah would be the bar manager, answering to Derrick, he would answer to Honey.

Sounded like a winner, and it gave her the freedom she needed to learn more about her new surroundings and spend more time with Jean Vincent when he was in town.

Then she got sick and threw up. She threw up her guts every morning the rest of the week until Hannah persuaded her to go the doctor. Surprise, surprise, she was pregnant.

Dear Diary:

"I must remind you, I am not a young girl. I am over thirty and am self-supporting. Yes, I have my beliefs, but they aren't hardcore religious, no particular church denomination, and I feel making love with a man who might be in my life forever, possibly as a husband, is acceptable. It is my choice. Whatever I chose to do sexually is all right as long as I don't hurt anybody else in the process. As a youth, a teenager, I was not indulgent in sex. Mama raised me properly, convinced me to save myself for marriage. But then after college and a few years out on my own, and no marriage, I decided to experiment and see what all the hullabaloo was about. By then I was an adult and making my own decisions and choices. I still am. So this is not Mama's fault.

"So here I am, just as Mama always feared. But this sudden interruption and revelation in my life isn't going to hurt anybody, not even me. I don't feel I am a sinner, is what I'm trying to say. Being a single mother is not a sin in my book, if that's what is in the cards for me. But there is a possibility that as soon as Jean Vincent returns, we will of

course be married.

"However I would never have thought this would happen to me, and it scares the shit out of me! What was I thinking? We didn't use protection, no birth control. What possessed me to skip that bit of smarts? Jeez! What a dummy!"

By the end of another month and no news of Jean Vincent, Honey's thoughts began to change. One moment it was: *I couldn't care less where he is.* The next moment it was: *He'll come back and we'll be married.* Then: *No. I won't try to get him to marry me just because I am pregnant. My mother did it alone, so will I. How dare he just disappear on me!*

One morning she woke up in the middle of the night sweating with anxiety. It had never occurred to her not to have the baby, to abort, or go to term and put the child up for adoption, no. Thoughts of her mama's experience and a school teacher friend of her mama's were on her mind that night before falling asleep.

She woke up as if lightning had struck her and she sat up in bed, the realization setting in. "I'm going to have a baby! A real baby!" She snapped on the lamp light and reached for her diary.

Dear Diary:

"When mama's friend Nola became pregnant and decided not to marry the father of the child, she carried the baby full term. Then after much consultation with family

and doctor, she decided to give up her child to a couple who wanted a son. They'd already adopted a girl and wanted a boy. Since Nola's family was made up of more boys than girls they thought she would be a good candidate to supply them with a son. The papers were signed and after all was said and done, Nola gave her newborn baby girl away.

"Although she didn't actually hand baby girl to them, and although she didn't see the baby at all, she knew it was a girl and she knew her name was Tami. And Nola's heart was broken.

"She fell into a deep depression for several months. Mama said she never got over it. Of course those around Nola didn't know what happened and the burden of guilt she was carrying. She was good at hiding it. One day Nola confided in mama because she felt mama would understand since she was a single mother. They became close friends after that. Mama's closest friend.

"On occasion as I was growing up, I would overhear their conversations, Nola telling mama there was a great part of her that was missing, and how she couldn't feel anything anymore. She would cry herself to sleep most nights. Even though she started dating again, she couldn't love anyone; although the self she portrayed to the world was a cheerful, fun-loving person. But she wouldn't open up to another man. She'd play the game, yes, but she wouldn't go beyond. It still hurt too much.

"I remember those conversations even now. Nola did marry and have other children, but she didn't stay long with her husbands. It was true, she couldn't give herself

completely, it wasn't there to give. Last I heard, she was retired, living alone, her children were grown with their own families, she didn't see them much. So sad."

Honey rubbed her flat belly, wondering when the baby would start showing and start moving. She began writing in the diary again:

"When Nola visited mama in the hospital they talked about her long lost daughter. Mama tried to convince her to look for the girl. She's an adult now and might want to know her birth mother, Mama said. Mama told Nola there would always be a tie between them, and if her daughter knew the truth, how much Nola had suffered, it might be the start of a healing process for both. That is, if the daughter knew she was adopted. Of course that could open up another whole can of worms. Nola was afraid."

Honey put the diary on the bedside table and laid her head back on the pillow. She was thinking how glad she was to be having her baby. She couldn't understand how anyone could give up a child. Now she would never be alone and someday she'd have grandchildren who would have children who would have children … on and on … never-ending.

She smiled and patted her belly, "I can do this, little fella," she said aloud.

12

It was one of those small train stations in Bulgaria that was lightly manned, and as the train departed it made a curve to the left and disappeared slowly through the tree and shrubbery tunnel that secluded a lot of the train routes in Europe. It was at that point Jean Vincent leapt from an overhanging tree branch onto the roof of the train. Although it looked simple to do, this was his second attempt of the day. The first one landed him along side the track with a bruised elbow. He had to wait for the next train.

Now he lay flat on its roof as the train continued towards the east coast of Bulgaria. Jean Vincent took advantage of his prone position to breathe easy and rest up before the next leg of his well-planned journey. As he lay there he thought of Honey, wondering for the umpteenth time how she had taken his phone call message – one he wouldn't want to receive, with no explanations. But he couldn't tell her any more than he had. He just hoped she would somehow trust him and believe he was coming back.

Just before nearing the border separating Bulgaria and Romania approaching the Black Sea, as the train slowed, he jumped from the roof and rolled into a ravine. He lay there trying to catch his breath knocked from him on impact. A hell of a way to travel, he was thinking. There had to be a better way, and he knew what it was. It was time to quit.

The Danube served as the separation line between Bulgaria and Romania with mountainous, forested land on both sides of the river, but Jean Vincent would bypass Romania on the Black Sea. He just had to make it to the craggy coast where contacts would be waiting on a fishing boat, moored just clear of the rocks.

His objective was to get to the Ukraine to rendezvous in Odessa with the other members of the team who were also getting there as best they could. Not leaving a trail of travel from one country to the next was vital for the mission. And the Black Sea was the shortest route from Bulgaria to the Ukraine. Each operative was on his own.

This was to be his last covert mission. No one knew it yet, but he had made the decision for himself; he would wait till this one was over and resign. Although the age of forty was still a reasonable age for players in his business, he had been at it since his early twenties, he figured the odds were stacking against him. Besides, now he had other interests.

13

It was one of those mornings, one of those sick throw up mornings. Honey couldn't believe she was on her knees with her head hovering over the toilet bowl, sick as a dog. The doctor told her it should be easing up, and it had nearly stopped until three days ago. All of a sudden it was as bad as it was at first. She sometimes felt that God was punishing her for fornicating out of wedlock. But then she couldn't see how that could be, she wasn't promiscuous, had only lain with Jean Vincent because she loved him and felt they might be heading for marriage. Although they didn't talk about it, she felt it could happen.

At the time Honey had no idea that Jean Vincent would suddenly disappear from her life. Wam-bam, thank you ma'am. How could God punish her under those circumstances? How could he be so cruel? She thought he was a loving God. So no, he wasn't punishing her. Of course, she knew she sort of jumped the gun, and she should have been on the pill. She wondered what her mama would say. Actually she knew what she would say. "Take the pill, girl, if you're going to bed him, take the pill!"

So here she was, four months pregnant, and she still hadn't heard from the baby daddy. But she was all right, she could do it herself. No problem.

She thought about Jean Vincent's parents, knowing they lived in Weymouth somewhere. *I wonder if I should try to find them and—no no no, I'm not going to do that.*

14

She didn't know what she would do without Hannah and Derrick and hoped they would never leave her. They were priceless.

Hannah was the most helpful person in the world. She not only knew the bar tending business, she knew all about babies and having them, had five sisters and they all had kids.

Derrick was such a wonderful man, helping Honey in every way he could. He drove her where she needed to go when she didn't feel well enough to drive, he took her shopping and carried all the bags into the house and put them away for her. He was always available to help her as well as run the business.

Just one shopping trip seemed to do her in lately, took her a couple days to recover from a day out. She was tired and her back hurt all the time, lower and upper. A burning hurt, like a tearing, ripping, she said.

Derrick gave her a back rub every time he came to the house. A sitting-up back rub, she wouldn't lie down, and she would be fully clothed.

Being six months pregnant was not fun. She felt awkward, clumsy, swollen and ugly. No one ever told her about that part of bringing a 'little miracle' into the world. It didn't feel much like a miracle to her.

She wondered if her mama felt the same. She wondered if Mama ever had second thoughts like she was having.

But it's too late now; I'm full into it, no turning back. "Oh, that feels so good, Derrick." Her eyes were closed as he worked his fingers up and down her spine.

"Lean forward a bit and I'll do your lower back. My mother always complained about her lower back pain, and being the only man around I would massage her while she watched TV at night."

"You were the only man around?" She didn't want to get too personal, but that piqued her interest.

"Oh yes. Only child, dead father."

"I'm so sorry. How old were you when he died?"

Derrick hesitated before answering. "Twelve."

"Then your mother raised you by herself?"

"Yes, she did. It wasn't easy, but she managed till I could go to work. I started out as a dishwasher and busboy, worked up to waiter and then front manager. Took a few years, but I was good at it, dedicated. Then I put myself through restaurant management school in London, landed some notable positions after that. So that's my life story in a nutshell."

He was grinning when Honey turned to look at him. "Would you like a cup of coffee, Derrick?"

"Yes, I would. Here, let me make it. You relax." He propped pillows behind and around her on the sofa.

"And your mother, Derrick, where does she live?"

"She died three years ago."

She felt so bad for asking. Sounded like he had a tough life. *Poor baby. I wonder how old he is. Looks about thirty or so, but seems younger.* "How old are you, Derrick?"

"Forty four."

"What? I would have thought you were younger than me." She couldn't believe it. Forty four? No way.

"Is that a bad thing? Being older than you?" he said with a wide grin.

"No, not really. You look so young. So why aren't you married with a passel of kids?"

"Oh, I guess I've been too busy."

Too many questions, she felt she was overstepping her boundaries and it was becoming uncomfortable. But it was amazing to her that he'd never married, a nice looking guy like him. You'd think he'd have several women after him. She wondered if Hannah was interested. She seemed to be very fond of him.

"Okay, I must get up from here and get busy. Thanks so much for the massage, Derrick. And thanks for taking me shopping."

"My pleasure. Anytime."

He stood and smiled at her, stared at her. It was a curious smile, endearing actually. Not overly wide and bright, just a nice simple, kind smile.

Her thoughts were: *He's nice. Not complicated, or so it seems. One never knows, though. Conscientious, serious, takes care of business.* "Okay, I must get something done around here," Honey said as she headed towards the kitchen.

"I'll be off, then. See you tomorrow." He went to the door and looked back at her before leaving, seeming to want to say something more.

"See you tomorrow, Derrick. Bright and early."

"Shall I pick you up in the morning?"

"No, no. I'll drive myself. Thanks for asking. Go on, go home. You don't have to attend me day and night." She laughed and waved him off.

"I don't mind," he said as he closed the door behind him.

Really nice guy. She turned and went into the kitchen.

15

"Hannah, do you have the schedule?" Honey asked while waddling through the front door of the pub. She didn't walk anymore, she waddled. The weight gain had been astronomical. Forty pounds. Unheard of. The doctor told her it would come off fast, not to worry. But she wasn't so sure of that. She'd never been fat in her entire life. This wasn't good.

"Yes, it's on the end of the bar. Over there," Hannah answered, pointing towards a black binder. "Shall I get it for you?"

"No. I'll get it. Thanks." Honey sat on the stool in front of the binder and opened it. "Okay, so Hillary won't be coming in today. She called me on my cell. Who can we bring in?"

"Janet is ready, she finished her training. And she's eager to get started. Shall I call her?"

"Yes, please do. Have you seen Derrick this morning?"

"He's upstairs. Said he's going to check the rooms to make sure they're clean. We've been having some trouble with the cleaning crew lately. He wants to sort it all out. If anybody can do it, he can. He's a love, isn't he?"

Honey looked at Hannah and saw that she was extraordinarily pretty that morning, more than usual. A new hairdo or new makeup, maybe both.

"You're looking great today, Hannah. Fabulous, in fact. What did you do that's different? I mean, I don't mean you don't look great all the time. Oh, you know what I mean."

Hannah laughed. "New hair color. Added some blond highlights. New color lipstick. You like it?"

"Yes, definitely! What a difference!" Honey wondered if she'd done it to attract Derrick.

"My sister talked me into it. She says I need to do a makeover and start exercising if I'm ever to meet Mr. Right."

"Oh? I didn't know you were looking."

"I'm always looking, ma'am, even at my age." She giggled. "I know he's out there. I'll find him."

"I figured you and Derrick might be an item."

"Oh no, Derrick's a good friend. Like a brother to me. We could never go there."

Okay, that answered Honey's question.

"Good morning!" Derrick came into the pub. "How are you feeling this morning, Honey?"

She never would get used to being called honey by a man in normal conversation, even though it was her name. "Feel pretty good, no aches or pains. Full of energy."

"Terrific! Well, I'm off to town. Anything I can pick up for you?" He grabbed his jacket from the coat rack.

Hannah reached for a piece of paper. "Here's the list for the bar."

"Nothing for me, Derrick. Got it all covered," Honey answered.

"Okay, be back in a couple hours. Cheerio!" Out the door he went.

Honey had hoped he'd hang around a while, have coffee with her. Lately she'd been looking forward to their coffee breaks and shopping excursions. It felt good to have a man around. Something she'd never had at any great length before.

Over the years she'd been pretty much independent, men weren't a part of her psyche - in the workplace, yes, but not personally. She had never felt there was room for one, till she met Jean Vincent. She figured she got that independence from her mother. Or maybe she learned it on her own, she was wondering about that now. Just the brief time she spent with Jean Vincent was out of the ordinary for her. Too bad her short-lived love affair wasn't reciprocal.

"You okay, Honey?" Hannah asked.

"Yes, what makes you ask?"

"You look a bit sad."

"Oh, I'm all right. Just thinking about the baby daddy."

"Have you heard anything from him?" Hannah frowned as she asked.

"Not a word."

"Didn't you say his folks live somewhere in Weymouth? Why don't you look them up?"

"No, no, no. I wouldn't do that. I'm not going to dump his mistake on them. My mistake. He left before I knew I was having this baby. Not his fault. So, no, not going there. I can do this myself."

16

Sunday was Honey's favorite day of the week. She liked to walk Weymouth harbor and have lunch at her favorite places, talk to the locals in the pubs. She had made quite a few friends since being there, coming up on eight months since she arrived. Not bad for her to be connecting to other people, so many so soon, very unlike her.

She figured there was something about Dorset that made her friendlier or calmer or whatever, maybe more receptive. Yes, that was it. She was more receptive, but it had to be because of the gracious people of Dorset. They made her feel that way.

She was meeting Martin and Ali for lunch on this particular Sunday at The Cove, out on the Portland strand of beach - Chesil Beach. She'd met them on one of her strolls before she gained so much weight. She didn't walk the promenade anymore because it was too difficult for her.

Derrick called and offered to drive her to Chesil Beach, but she said no, she could manage. He insisted and wouldn't let up till she finally gave in. No harm in him going. After all, she thought it might be fun with him along.

Martin and Ali were such talkers and she adored them, was looking forward to Sunday lunch with them again. They always had the latest promenade gossip, being the owners of the Channel View B & B. Their own stories were very interesting too. Honey loved hearing how they had met and ended up in Weymouth, and finally married in Hawaii. Good friends they were becoming to her.

Oh there he is! Honey saw him pull up when she looked out of the bay window. She opened the front door and yelled, "I'll be right there, Derrick. No need to come up to the house."

She thought he looked great in his navy blue sweater and jeans. Blond hair shining looked like he just shampooed it, clean and fresh. Not a bad looking guy.

"Are you sure? Do you need me to carry anything?"

She came through the doorway. "No, just me and purse today. I'm traveling light." *And there he goes, opening the car door for me. Such a gentleman. Nice guy, yes he is.*

"Thank you for letting me come along, Honey. I was restless today, needed to do something. My day off can be rather boring. How are you feeling?"

"I'm good. Just a little sore from all the kicking this child is doing, but my back is okay today." She watched as Derrick walked around to his door and joined her in the car.

"Well, when I bring you home, if your back is l hurting, I'll work on it for you."

She could not believe a man could be so perceptive and willing. One thing for sure, there weren't many like him. Two days prior he had called and said he'd found a basinet that was on sale and had bought it. He wanted to bring it over. It was lovely. Was decorated in white and yellow dotted Swiss and had a full layette with it. Honey couldn't believe it!

"So you've known Martin and Ali since you've been here?"

She looked over at Derrick as he drove towards Wyke Regis on the way to Portland. "I met them a few days after I got here on one of my evening walks along the promenade. They were sitting outside their B & B, drinking wine. I stopped to talk to them, and then I ran into them at the George Inn one night and we've been friends ever since."

"Which B & B?" he asked.

"The Channel View, across from the Mandarin restaurant on the beach."

"Ah, yes, one of my favorite restaurants. We'll have to go there sometime." He glanced at her, wanting a response.

Honey didn't say anything. They rode in silence the rest of the way.

17

Sunday Lunch at The Cove was as special as always. The first time Honey went there was with Ali and Martin and had been there several times since.

Derrick fit right in. He was cordial to anybody he met, one of the best things Honey liked about him. Even at the pub in Abbotsbury he was a hit and drew in new customers every week. Honey felt lucky to have him on staff.

"So, Derrick, where did you work in London?" Martin asked as he sipped his beer standing at the bar waiting on a table for the four of them.

"At the Triangle first, was bar manager there for a time. Then moved to Jason Priest's new restaurant where I was general manager. Worked in hotels too, front and back office. Last place I was a GM at a small hotel near Green Park. Right in the middle of the big ones."

"So how is he working out in Abbotsbury, Honey?"

"Couldn't be better, Ali, honest. I don't know what I would have done without him. I keep saying that, I know. Thanks to Hannah for bringing him on."

"I was fortunate that Hannah told me about the place, and fortunate you hired me."

The barkeep interrupted them and took them to a table in the dining area.

After they were seated and ordered, Martin asked Honey, "So what do you hear from Jean Vincent?"

She went pale and blank for a moment. Derrick jumped in and answered for her. "He hasn't contacted her yet, but he will. He said he would when he got to where he was going."

She couldn't believe what Derrick said to her friends, running interference for her. "I wonder how long it takes for a person to find out where they're going? He's been gone for months." Honey took a deep breath and added, "So it appears he has found something else to do besides be in my life. And it's okay. It really is. I've accepted it. I can do this. My mother did it, so can I. So, no problem. I just find it ironic that I'm here living in my mama's lover's house, running his business, and they're both dead – mama and papa. And even more ironic that I met a man exactly where mama met my papa and I'm about to have his baby out of wedlock. Another single mother. Unbelievable, isn't it?" Tears came to her eyes; she grabbed her purse and made straightway to the ladies room. Saying it out loud made it more real.

"Has she tried to find Jean Vincent's parents? I

understand they live further down the promenade from us," Ali said.

"Maybe we should do some asking around, not tell her we're doing it," Martin added.

Derrick took a sip of his beer. "I think that would be a good idea. Shouldn't be hard to find them. The time will come when they'll need to know they have a grandchild. If nothing else she needs closure. So if you find out anything, let me know, and I'll take it from there."

They all agreed.

"Do you know the history of this pub, Derrick?" Martin was asking as Honey returned to the table. The food had been served and they were eating.

"No, I don't. I haven't been here long enough, never been in this part of England before."

"Well, before the Cove House, there were three fishermen cottages on this site. This particular building dates back to the early nineteenth century, but there were earlier versions back to the late seventeenth and early eighteenth centuries. So it's been here for a long while."

Honey reached for a glass of water.

"Are you okay, Honey?" Ali asked.

"Yes, yes, I am. I'm fine now. Derrick, something I find interesting about the Cove, it played a big part during the influx of storms and shipwrecks on this coastline, and was used for treating survivors."

"Is that right?"

Martin added, "Yes, and storms are still pretty lethal here. The water can top the 49-foot high Chesil Beach, that's the name of this beach actually. They built it that high to protect the village. But it can be dangerous out here. You see those mesh baskets of stones? They are stacked up to hold the ridge of the beach. Works most of the time. But a couple times the sea smashed into the pub as well as tossed stones onto the roof."

"Martin knows his history," Ali said, "and he's hooked on historical fiction."

"He knows his dates too," Honey added. "He told me last time we came that they had to close the pub for three months in 1989 when a storm hit and did tons of damage. Don't you just love the history of these places? Can't you just imagine that happening?" She glanced at Derrick to see if he was getting bored. She loved talking about historic places, but not everybody felt the same.

"Yes, the history captivates me, Honey," Martin said. "You can read and research for days and you'll never know all there is to know about Dorset."

Honey raised her glass and signaled the barkeep, "I'll have another, please."

"I'll get it for you." Derrick was being the gentleman once again.

"So what are you writing these days, Honey?" Ali asked.

"Oh just some short stories. I haven't had the focus to write another novel. In the meantime I write short stories, mostly flash fiction, an exercise actually. But once in a while a good story comes out of it and then I develop it into a novel."

"Here's your wine. What is flash fiction?" Derrick asked.

Honey took the drink. "It's fiction that is very, very short, micro fiction. Some people call it post-card fiction. The stories can be as little as three-hundred words up to a thousand, very short."

"That's interesting. I'd love to read some of your stories, if you'll let me. I didn't know that about you."

"Well, I don't talk about it much, Derrick. Hasn't been uppermost in my mind lately." She patted her belly. "This little fella is taking up my days, along with the business. Not much time for writing."

"I hope I'm alleviating some of the business pressures for you."

"Oh that you are. Definitely. Hey, like I've said a jillion times, I don't know what I'd do without you." She took another sip of her drink. "Okay, this is the second glass, no more for me today. I have one or two glasses a week. The doc said that shouldn't hurt the baby. Oh boy, he's kicking me now! Can you see it?"

18

The dinghy cut through the water, racing towards Jean Vincent. He'd been signaling his team mates from shore for nearly half an hour before they spotted him. A day late from the scheduled rendezvous time, he had been worried they wouldn't wait for him. But they did.

Safe onboard the sleek 16m boat, approximately 53 feet, Jean Vincent took a few deep breaths and tried to relax. His heart wasn't in this anymore. All he wanted to do was go back to England and be with Honey.

"What's the problem? You aren't yourself," Vllad, his trusted friend, asked him.

"No problem. My mind is elsewhere."

"You have second thoughts about this?" Taodis asked him.

"I will be honest with you, yes I am questioning. But I will finish this and it will be the last for me." Jean

Vincent headed to the galley for coffee.

The other four men glanced at each other, Vllad frowning, Taodis, sitting on the cushioned bench, leaning back against the railing, rubbing his face with both hands; the other two sitting, shaking their heads.

"This is not good," Taodis said. 'Doubt is not good."

Suddenly off to the starboard, a gunner boat appeared bearing down upon them. They all saw it at the same time and panic set in.

"Go, go, Serge!" Vllad called out to the captain who was at the center console.

Jean Vincent appeared from the galley and walked into the shouts and commotion. "What is it?" he shouted.

"Patrol boat. Get down into the galley. Everybody, go!"

"But they've already seen us," Taodis called out as he reached the stairway. "They must have seen us pick up Jean Vincent. Someone tipped them off."

"No matter. Out of sight." Vllad was standing, machine gun ready on the bench at his knees.

Serge revved the triple Mercury Verado 300 HP outboard motors and within a few seconds was racing north towards Ukraine territory. His boat was made to look like a modern, pleasure fishing vessel, but it was a high-powered racing boat. He not only used it to take out groups of executives on holiday, but was also available for covert ops when needed.

Serge knew they would be safe in the Ukraine port of Odessa, since he and his boat were registered there and he could convince the patrollers that he was a legitimate fishing vessel, with a group of avid fishermen aboard. All five men spoke fluent Russian. He just needed to get closer to Odessa.

With an AKA sub machine gun Jean Vincent stood on the galley stairs, visible to Vllad, but not to the aggressors. Serge was armed as were the other three men waiting in the hole behind Jean Vincent.

Ahead of the racer another patrol boat rushed towards them attempting to cut off their escape to safe waters.

The boat that was previously at their starboard was now at their stern and firing which prompted the boat at their bow to pelt them with rounds too.

All five men on the fishing boat fired at will while Serge tried his best to head for the beach in an attempt to outrun the onslaught of inevitable doom and death.

19

A pain shot through Honey's abdomen. She bent over, holding her belly.

Hannah saw her fall to the side on the sofa by the fireplace where she had been reading the monthly report given her by Derrick. "Are you all right?" she called out to Honey while she replaced a bottle on the bar-back.

"I don't know. Oh! There it is again. Must be gas. Ow! Another. That one hurt!" She looked pale suddenly, doubled over pressing her face against the seat cushion.

"I'll get Derrick!" Hannah said, running up the stairs towards the office.

Honey lay writhing on her side as harsh pains below her ribs emanated across her back and belly.

"What is it?" Derrick shouted as he ran towards her. "Are you still having pains?"

"Yes," Honey said breathlessly. "Something's wrong. I don't think it's gas this time."

"Okay, we're off to hospital. Hannah, fetch her coat and purse, please."

At hospital Honey was diagnosed with pre-eclampsia. She tested high blood pressure and there was protein in her urine. Those combined with the pain were three signs of the condition. She was put on a drip of sulfate magnesium to assist in preventing her from developing full eclampsia, if that was what it was. Eclampsia is a severe illness that could inflame the brain membranes and put her and the baby at risk, even death. The doctors felt they had caught it early enough but were keeping her in hospital to control fluid levels and monitor her blood pressure.

Later it was decided she should stay in hospital till her baby was born, one way or another; they discussed Caesarean birth and induced labor as possibilities if she didn't improve. She told them saving the baby was the most important, so she would go along with whatever it took.

During the next two weeks she did well, the blood pressure was regulated and her fluid level was controlled. But the two weeks in confinement made her extremely antsy. She picked up her cell phone and called Ali.

"Honey, how are you? I'll be there later this evening, we have a late check-in. Is that all right?"

"You needn't come every day. I don't want to foul

up your lives." But regardless she was thrilled to hear Ali was coming.

"But I want to. I mean, I don't want to foul up my life, and I'm not," she laughed. "I want to come see you. Martin is coming too. So is Derrick. We have something to talk to you about, and we're bringing a surprise."

"Oh? What is it? Tell me, tell me. I can't wait. You didn't go out and buy me a bunch of baby stuff, did you? Don't do that. Promise me you didn't."

Ali frowned and looked over at Martin sitting at his desk. "I'll tell you when we get there, Okay? See you then." She hung up quickly.

Martin leaned back in his chair. "I don't know. Do you think we should? Do you think this is the right time?"

"The doctor said the best time is now while she can be monitored. Yes, it's for the best." But Ali wasn't a hundred percent certain.

20

Honey lay in the hospital bed thinking of the past year and all that had happened since her mother handed her the Christmas diary the night she died - telling her about her father.

She turned on her side in the bed, and faced the window that opened to the hospital grounds. The twinkling Christmas lights in the trees gave the garden an ethereal glow.

Her eyes filed with tears; a few trickled to her pillow. She wasn't feeling sorry for herself, not at all. She missed her mama. She wished she could be there to see her grandchild. Mama would have loved that, and so would her papa.

Honey decided that one way to pay homage to her mother and show her gratefulness was to raise her own child without a father too. Maybe others wouldn't see it that way, but it didn't matter, that's what she wanted. She'd already decided. It wasn't the ideal; she always said she would never deprive a child of hers of a father. But even if Jean Vincent returned, she decided she would do it without him.

Reaching for her diary on the bedside stand, she sat up and began writing:

Dear Diary:

"In spite of the pain and the hopelessness I feel, I still am grateful I am having this precious child. I prefer not to know if it is a girl or boy before its birth, I'm open to either, and will love and adore it no matter what it is. One day I will give these diaries to my baby to read, when he or she is old enough, just like mama did to me. But I won't make the mistake of not telling him from the beginning about Jean Vincent, I won't wait till the diaries are read.

"I will add here, however, that at the moment I'm a bit aggravated and am feeling that Jean Vincent wasn't very thoughtful to just take off and never contact me without a word in all these months. But aside from that, while we were together I loved him, and I think he loved me. So I can't deny ... in that love our baby was conceived. No better way for a being to start a life, his parents loving each other. I have no regrets in that respect.

"I feel sorry for the mothers carrying children who don't want them or who are incapable of or have an aversion to caring for them after they're born. The neglect and cruelty those dear sweet, innocent children are

subjected to, through no fault of their own, burdens my heart so much. There's too much pain in this world between unwanted children and those who bore them in lust, stupor, poverty, and crime. I just can't go there in my mind, it is too horrible, and my heart is heavy for those children.

"One thing I do know is that I promise to create a world for my child that will make him feel loved and wanted, and he will know he can do whatever he wants in life. She or he, whatever the case may be. My mother gave that same promise to me."

"Knock knock," Ali said with a big grin as she opened the door to Honey's hospital room and peeked in.

"Come in, come in." Honey placed her diary in the top drawer of the night stand.

"Surprise! We brought you Thanksgiving Dinner. I baked the turkey myself. Martin did the mashed potatoes and gravy. Are you hungry?"

Martin moved the hospital tray on wheels closer to Honey. "That should do it. Look what else we brought," he said looking towards the open doorway.

Derrick came 'round the corner carrying Champagne and flowers. "Brought some ginger ale for you, but the real stuff is for us."

They were all cheerful, full of grins and laughter.

Ali took the roses and found a vase, added water and set them on the bedside table.

"Those are so pretty, thank you very much. All of you, thanks for all of this. I didn't figure I'd get Thanksgiving dinner in the UK." She laughed. "Sure looks good." She picked up the fork and scooped up the green beans. "Yum yum." Then she tried the dressing. "I can't believe how good this tastes! Wow! Who cooked the dressing?"

Martin raised his hand. "I did, love. The recipe was on the box."

"Doesn't taste like any box dressing I've ever had."

"Well, I added some of my own herbs and vegetables. Couldn't just let it be plain, could I?"

Derrick handed paper cups of bubbly all around. "We had our dinner before we came, so it's time for us to drink while you eat. Cheers!"

"Cheers!" They all resounded.

"This is so good. I didn't know I was so hungry," Honey said as she made quick haste in eating the food. "Didn't you say you had something to tell me?"

Martin and Derrick glanced at Ali.

"Honey, we have some good news for you first. We found Jean Vincent's parents. As it turns out they live right down the promenade from us. Their house faces the sea. We've walked by there hundreds of times, I'm sure you have too." Ali took a deep breath. "And we told them about you and the baby. And— "

Ali frowned and looked away. She put her hand over her mouth.

Martin touched Ali's shoulder. "They told us that Jean Vincent had a terrible accident, Honey. "On the Black Sea not far from Romania and wasn't recovered. Said they received a phone call from someone in Paris a few days ago saying he was lost at sea."

Honey dropped her fork on the plate and fell back on the pillows, her eyes wide and stoic. Her mind and heart stopped.

Derrick took her hand. "Take it easy, Honey. Think of the baby. You're all right. They said he had never been gone that long without calling them and they had been worried, knew something had to have happened. So they made calls to people he knew in Paris and someone who knew what happened finally called them."

Martin spoke up, "His parents want to meet you, Honey. We told them you would have to make that decision, and we would let them know one way or another."

"Where's my drink?" Honey asked, sitting up straight in the bed.

"Here it is." Derrick handed it to her.

Honey put her hand up in protest, "No, I want the real stuff," she said. "What was he doing on the Black Sea, for God's sakes? Does anybody know? What was he doing there? He said he was taking care of business in Paris. What was he doing in that Godforsaken part of the world? What the hell?" Tears spilled down her cheeks as her chin quivered.

Ali touched her shoulder, "Sweetie, calm down, please calm down. We're all sad that he's gone, we are. But you need to think of the baby now. This is a critical time for the baby. You shouldn't upset yourself."

Honey thought for a couple seconds, then reached for a tissue and wiped her eyes and nose. "You're right. Just had a moment there. Of course you're right." She reached for the ginger ale. "I'll pretend this is the real thing. Cheers!"

But the heart pain was still brewing in her eyes, she fooled nobody.

21

"Brought you a present!" Derrick said, bursting into Honey's hospital room unannounced. "No flowers this time ... something more lasting." He handed a pink gift bag to her.

"Well, hello to you too," she said with eyes wide and a grin spreading across her face. "What is this?"

"Look and see." He pulled up a chair to the side of her bed.

She dipped her hand through the curly ribbons piled in the bag filled with tissue paper and pulled out a long narrow, white box. Her thoughts jumped to bracelet or watch, it was that size gift box.

"Derrick, you shouldn't have done this."

"Open it, and yes I should, better yet ... I wanted to."

She lifted the lid and stared. "Oh my gosh! It's a

diamond tennis bracelet. This is beautiful, Derrick! You can't do this."

"Too late, it's done! Like I said I wanted to do it. You deserve it, Honey. If you have a girl, it'll be an heirloom to give her when she grows up. I love stuff like that. Here, let me fasten it on you." He reached for the bracelet and opened the clasp.

Still stunned, Honey held out her arm. She couldn't get over what a gem Derrick was, speaking of gems. "Are these real diamonds? I mean, it's okay if they aren't, in fact, I hope they aren't."

"They're real, and so is the gold. I wouldn't buy you a fake anything. There. You're all set."

She twisted her wrist and watched the diamonds and gold glisten in the sunlight that was streaming through the bedside windows. "I just love it! I do. Thank you so much. Come here, I need to give you a thank you kiss, at least."

Derrick leaned over and their lips met briefly. They both were flustered for a second, and then continued on a bit too fast with conversation about pub business.

A while later, a nurse came through the doorway carrying a tray. "Lunchtime, Honey. Oh, shall I set another tray for you, Derrick?"

"No, no, I've got lunch plans, Amy. I just wanted to stop by and go over some things with Honey."

"Look what he brought me." Honey lifted her arm as she beamed with pride. "I've never had a tennis bracelet. I wonder why they call it that."

A tiny, wiry woman, Amy touched the bracelet. "That is a beauty, isn't it? I heard that the term began back in the eighties when Chris Everett was wearing a thin line diamond bracelet and it broke while she was playing. They had to stop the game and find the diamonds. After that it became a fad, thin diamond bracelets worn by tennis players. I'm a tennis fan, so my husband bought me one for Christmas one year, but I'm sure mine is Cubic Zirconias, CZs my daughter calls them." She laughed. "But the sentiment is there, doesn't matter what they are, do you agree?"

"Absolutely, you are so right; it's the sentiment that counts." Honey glanced at Derrick, while caressing her bracelet and still feeling the soft touch of his lips.

"Okay, there you are, Missy. I'm off to serve lunch to the others. Is there anything else I can get you?"

"No, that'll do. Thank you."

Derrick stood and placed the chair back against the wall. "Well, I must get on with it. I've got things to do this afternoon before going back to the Inn. Are you all right? Need any books or magazines? Supplies? Anything?"

"No no, nothing. Ali brings me toiletries, so I'm full up with those. Don't need any books or mags … I've been writing, mostly. Plenty of time to do that now. I'll be so glad when I'm out of here. This isn't my style at all." Honey pushed away the bed tray on wheels.

"Here let me do that for you," Derrick said and positioned it over the foot of the bed.

"Thanks. And thank you again for this beautiful bracelet. Now I'm hoping I'll have a girl more than ever."

She laughed.

"If you do, what will you name her? Have you picked any names yet?" Derrick sat on the edge of the bed, holding file folders to his chest.

"Oh, I don't know, I think I'll wait and see. I'll let the name fit the child, that's what some people do, I hear. My mother did that. Of course, I wish she would have named me something else, mine is ridiculous. I won't do that to my daughter, if it's a daughter."

They both laughed.

"I'm grateful my parents didn't name me Earl Derrick. Can you imagine the laughs I'd get from my school chums?"

"That's funny. You mean oil Derrick? That would have been awful." Honey laughed.

Derrick stood, "Yes, I agree. Well, cheerio! I must be going. I'll see you tomorrow, if not tonight."

22

Early one morning on his rounds the doctor told Honey the baby was healthy and everything looked normal, said it was a just matter of days till she would deliver.

At first she panicked. She wasn't ready. Honey's moods shifted up and down, from one day to the next, from one minute to the next. One moment she was sad and depressed that Jean Vincent wasn't there, or she wondered if she was doing the right thing keeping the baby, the next moment she was glad to be having it and was excited beyond belief. She knew she could raise the child by herself. Her mama did it. She kept telling it to herself.

She wondered just how much her mama clung to the memories of her papa in those days, and how much she thought of him. Did she think of him every day? She hadn't read all the diaries yet, and only the year before Honey was born contained the most mention of her papa so far.

But what she did remember was that her mama showed nothing but glee and happiness with Honey as far back as she could remember. She was always attentive and loving, never seemed to begrudge being a single mother. Never complained. Maybe God was giving Honey the experience so she'd know what her mother went through. Honey settled for that reasoning more and more as the days went by.

"Well, one thing for sure," she told herself, "I'll always tell my child about its daddy, and I will not name it a silly name like mine."

That was the plan.

"Have you decided about meeting Jean Vincent's parents?" Ali asked Honey that afternoon when she arrived with a package of baby blankets and disposable diapers.

"I think it will be all right, don't you? After all they're the grandparents. The only grandparents my baby will have. I mean ... it isn't fair that a child be deprived of its grandparents." Her spirits were unusually high in that moment. "I love those blankets. Let me feel them."

Ali handed one of them to her and set the others on the empty bed behind them.

"Oh! Ouch! Omigod!" Honey bent towards her knees. "I've having a terrible pain, Ali. God! Oh my God! It's getting worse. It hurts! Oh no!"

"I'll call the nurse!" Ali ran from the room into the hall.

Honey could hear her calling out for help. She turned on her side and pulled her knees up. "This can't be the baby, can it?" she said aloud, screaming out to whoever was listening. "It can't be. Not yet. Oh! It's making me sick! I'm getting sick. Help, somebody!"

Nurse Amy and doctor rushed in.

Honey's blood pressure and all the vital signs were at safe levels, the pre-eclampsia was still under control, no problem there.

"It's beginning," the calm, smiling doctor told her. "Labor is beginning. Your baby will be here anywhere from ten to twenty hours from now. There's nothing to worry about. You and the baby will be fine."

Ali was caressing Honey's hand as the doctor talked to her.

"Wait! I feel like liquid is coming out of me. Am I bleeding?" She began to cry as she looked up at him, terrified. "Am I?"

Amy raised the cover and checked her. "Her water's broken, doctor."

He put one hand on Honey's forehead and reached for her hand with the other. "Just relax, my dear. This is normal. The baby is protected in a sac of fluid during your pregnancy, when he is about to be born, the sack membranes burst and his journey begins. It's perfectly normal. Amy will clean you up and you'll be good as new. Baby is eager to meet his mother, sooner than we thought. So don't panic, just breathe slow and easy and go with it. Stay calm." He turned to the nurse. "I'll be in my office." He left the room.

"I better call Martin and Derrick, be right back. Will you be all right, Honey?" Ali frowned as she saw the fear on Honey's face and was hoping it wasn't a refection of her own. "I promise, be right back," She kissed Honey's forehead and hurried to the reception area to make the calls.

Nurse Amy closed the door behind Ali. "Okay, let's clean you up," she said. She changed Honey's wet gown and replaced the wet bed pad with a dry one. She assured her that this was normal and it wasn't a complication, this happened to every mother in labor. Then she explained what would happen next, how the pains would increase and the duration between pains would be shorter and shorter till time to birth.

Honey was scared to death and she was feeling so alone, totally alone. "Can you give me something to stop the pain? It's horrible!"

"No no no. You can do this." Amy went into the bathroom to dampen a fresh cloth with warm water. She returned to bedside and gently wiped Honey's forehead and face. "I need to do a quick exam, my dear, to check for cervical dilation. It'll be uncomfortable for you, but try and relax as best you can." She put on a rubber glove and then folded the covers aside. "Raise your knees and spread them apart, please."

"So what does this do? Will it hurt?"

"Try to relax, Honey. That's it. What happens is during the late stages of pregnancy your cervix may have already dilated from one to three centimeters, I'm checkin' that now, to see if it's more." She talked while she examined to distract Honey. "During actual labor the uterine contractions will widen your cervix up to six centimeters. And then in the final stage of labor, when the baby is there knocking at the door, the pressure from his head will cause the softened cervix to widen up to ten centimeters."

This frightened Honey even more. "Ten centimeters?" She began to cry. "I can't do this, I can't!"

"Yes you can, this is a good thing, sweetie. Think of all the women before you who have done it – millions and millions. You're a brave one. Before you know it, your dear little angel will be in your arms and the contractions and pain will disappear. It will be as if it never happened. Funny thing about that, our minds have a way to set the memory aside, or cloud it a bit, else we'd never have another child, would we? So it'll be over before you know it. Trust me. Just go with the flow. The good Lord wouldn't give us pain we couldn't endure."

"I'll never have another baby. That's for sure. Here comes another pain! Oh no! Do you have any children?" Honey asked, trying to get her mind off what was happening.

"I have four of 'em. So see, the pain didn't stop me, I kept poppin' 'em out one after another. Okay, that's it for the exam. You're up to a four."

"It's getting worse. Oh! Oh! It feels like a hard cramp, a burning sick pain spreading across my back and coming across my tummy. Omigod! It makes me want to fold up. This one really hurts. Ohhhhh ... I can't— "

There was a knocking at the door.

The nurse opened it and Ali hurried to Honey's

bedside, taking her hand. "Sorry I took so long, couldn't get hold of them at first. Are you all right?"

With tears in her eyes looking up at Ali, Honey whispered hoarsely, "I can't do this ... "

23

Honey's baby girl arrived twenty hours later on December 24 at eight a.m., missing her mother's exact birthday, six hours earlier. Still a Christmas baby, though, a beautiful little angel born on Christmas Eve morning.

Honey slept till four p.m., awoke when the maternity nurse came in to bring the baby for her first breast feeding. It took a few minutes to figure it all out, but Honey adapted quite quickly, better than most.

Her heart overflowed with love and affection for the little creature in her arms. She couldn't believe this tiny being was hers to hold and protect for years to come. This was the real deal. Her own child.

As she looked at every inch of her precious little baby, she was mesmerized at the softness and glow of its skin. Not a blemish or a wrinkle, tiny lips that were perfect, miniature fingers and toes, black hair, twinkling dark blue eyes. The nurse told her the eyes might change color.

"I know what I'm going to name you, my little Christmas baby." Honey kissed her forehead, smelling her sweetness.

24

Derrick arrived first that evening, carrying pink roses for the new mother, his eyes were reddened as if he'd been crying. "I saw her, and she's so lovely. Such a little thing, so helpless. She was sleeping with her tiny rosebud mouth puckered." Grinning from ear to ear, he handed the flowers to Honey. "How are you? You feeling all right?"

"Oh yes, I feel wonderful. Truly. A bit achy and sore, but I'm recovering nicely, pains are gone. These are beautiful, Derrick." She buried her nose in the blossoms, then handed them back to Derrick. "Would you mind putting them in some water, in that vase over there?"

"Of course." He did as he was told, gladly. "Hannah said to give you her love, she'll come tomorrow morning," Derrick said in a loud voice from the bathroom.

"Martin and Ali called, said they'd be a little late," Honey adjusted her pillows so she could sit up straighter.

He came back to her bed carrying the vase of blossoms. "Mr. and Mrs. Doucet will be coming with them. They did tell you, right?" He set the roses on the night stand, then pulled up a chair facing her.

"No, they didn't. But I don't have a problem with that. What are they like?" She spread the covers smoothly across her body, noticing the absence of a pregnant bump for the first time.

"They're nice people. You'll like them, I'm sure you will. And they are excited about having a grandchild; you can imagine how they must feel – losing a son, gaining a grandchild. But before they get here, I've brought you a present." He reached into his coat pocket and took out a small ribboned box and handed it to her.

"You already gave me the wonderful bracelet, I don't need another gift. What is it?" She turned it over and over in her hands.

Derrick laughed. "Well, open it and find out."

She untied the ribbon and lifted the lid. "What is this?" In the box were two matching rings of blue topaz, a lady's ring and a child's ring. There were three small stones in a row on the child's ring, but on the lady's ring there was a large topaz in the middle, one smaller stone on each side of it.

"For two very special friends of mine. Happy Birthday!"

With tears in her eyes and a strong feeling of gratitude and affection, Honey reached for him.

He leaned over for the loving hug she gave him and gave her one in return. He looked into her eyes and said, "Honey, I— "

But before he could finish, Ali and Martin came through the door.

"Oh, I see we've been beaten out by our friend Derrick, he gets to hug you first? We can't have that now, can we?" Ali laughed and headed straight for Honey, first setting Christmas presents on the foot of the bed, then hugging her. "How are you, sweetie? You all right?"

"I am. I am. So glad you came back."

Martin led Jean Vincent's parents into the room. They placed their winter coats on a chair. "

"Honey, this is Josef and Marie Doucet," Martin said. "We've just come from viewing the baby."

Josef Doucet was an older version of Jean Vincent with grey streaks in his coal black hair. Seeing him brought tears to Honey's eyes, memories that were never far from the surface. Marie Doucet was a tiny woman, well-dressed and elegant in a white winter suit. A lovely lady.

Josef spoke up first, "We are so happy to meet you." He leaned forward and took Honey's hand as he did the European two-cheek kiss. "I am sorry we didn't meet while our son was here. It has been a sad time for us. This makes it much better."

His wife, Marie, placed two beautifully wrapped gifts next to the others on the bed and extended her hand to Honey as Josef stepped back. "You are so lovely, my dear, and so soon after childbirth." She too kissed Honey. "Your daughter is just as lovely as you. Congratulations."

Honey was doing all she could to keep from crying. "You'll have to forgive me; this is all a bit overwhelming. You are my baby's only grandparents. Both my parents are gone, just this last year. So you can't imagine how happy I am for you wanting to be part of our lives. Thank you so much!" She wiped her eyes with tissue from the side table.

Derrick clutched her shoulder gently, then sat beside her on a chair he had pulled close to the bed.

"Now that you all are here, I want to announce the name of our little angel, are you ready for this?"

"Yes, yes," Derrick said quickly, as he took the tissue from Honey and dropped it in the waste basket. "I've been waiting for this moment."

"Us too," Ali said. "Oh! This is exciting!"

Martin pulled up two more chairs on the opposite side of the bed for Ali and Marie, they sat, the men stood.

"Okay, I'm going to call her ... Eve ... because she was born on Christmas Eve and because my mama's middle name was Evelyn. I'm still not sure of Eve's middle name though."

Derrick grinned widely. "How about Noel? Eve Noel?"

"Oh my goodness! I love it, Derrick! That is perfect. Eve Noel. Christmas Eve." She giggled and grinned at Derrick, squeezing his hand and looking into his eyes. "You're so clever."

They all agreed it was a divine name for an exquisite little creature.

"Oh, I ... I just love you all!"

Rebecca Buckley

"We love you too," Derrick said softly and kissed her cheek.

The nurse brought in the baby and placed her in Honey's arms.

Martin and Ali stood close together, Martin's arm around Ali, looking on at the blessings of a very special Christmas Eve. They glanced over at the Doucets who at that moment kissed each other in happiness.

If a picture postcard had been created of the moment, if a photo would have been snapped, it would have shown a beaming Derrick, sitting next to Honey, his hand on her shoulder, looking down at baby Eve Noel nestled in Honey's arms. It would have shown four other loving guardians leaning over and gazing at the sleeping child. Oh and we must not forget the beautifully wrapped gifts in the foreground.

A perfect picture, a Christmas card scene that was reminiscent of another glorious Christmas event many, many years ago.

25

Dear Diary:

"My sweet Eve Noel is five years old today. We're giving her a birthday party this afternoon. Granma and Granpa Doucet will be here at four with a new little puppy. Eve Noel has wanted a puppy of her very own because Derrick's two, big dogs just don't do the trick for her, she says. She's been saying she wants a little-bitty puppy for a little-bitty girl. And wouldn't you know, she crooks her finger and everybody jumps. They're bringing her a Maltese puppy.

"I just love my precious little bundle. I cannot believe she's five years old. How did that happen so quickly?

"Derrick has been a wonderful husband and father, I couldn't have asked for a better person in either case, and he manages the business perfectly. How did I get so lucky?

I love him with all my heart, and I thank God every day that Eve Noel has a daddy. A mommy and a daddy, that's what she calls us. The Doucets are unbelievably kind and considerate to Derrick; they treat him like a son. They love our little daughter.

"I think of Jean Vincent from time to time, I remember how much I loved him, and I miss him. I wonder about his death. We never have been satisfied with the explanations given. But that is behind us, those days are gone and it all happened for a reason. I know I must think only of today and be open and ready to what's in store for us tomorrow.

"I've written five diaries of my own, Mama, just like you did. And one day I'll give Eve Noel her own Christmas diary, just as you gave me.

"I think of you always, my dear mama and papa. Every single day. I love and miss you so very much."

Luke 2:13-14 And suddenly there was with the angel a multitude of the heavenly host praising God and saying, "Glory to God in the highest, and on earth peace among those with whom he is pleased!"

Also by Rebecca Buckley

NOVELS - Rachel O'Neill Series

Midnight at Trafalgar
Midnight at the Eiffel
Midnight in Brussels
Midnight in Moscow
Midnight in Malibu
Midnight in Vegas – coming in 2014

COLLECTIONS - Stories and Plays

Love Has a Price Tag
Bits & Pieces of Me
My Dramedy
Shoe's on the Other Foot

You may contact Rebecca at:
www.rebeccabuckley.com
rebeccajbuckley@aol.com